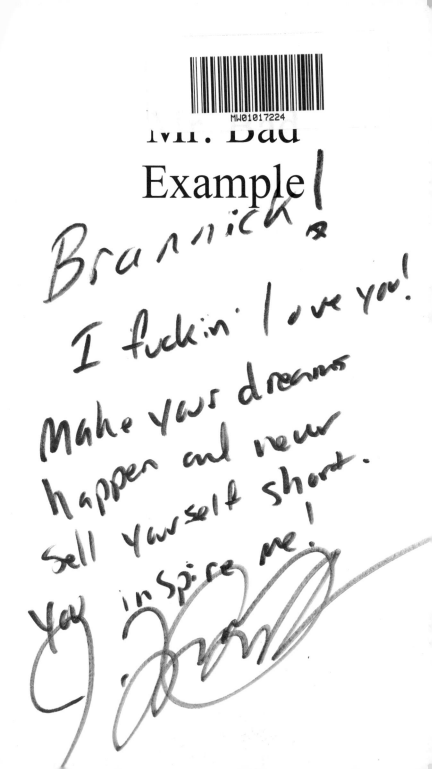

MW01017224

Mr. Bad
Example!

Brannick!

I fuckin' love you!

Make your dreams
happen and never
sell yourself short.
You inspire me!

Mr. Bad Example

A Novel By:

J. Travis Grundon

Insomnious Press, 2013

ISBN:148126107X
ISBN-13:978-1481261074

for the one that didn't get away

ACKNOWLEDGMENTS

Huge thanks to the following people:

Stormi Gilliatt, for putting up with me and putting a smile on my face.

Rebecca and Michael Mullen, for everything they do.

James M. Bowers and everyone at Insomnious Press, and B.C. Brown and everyone in the Vincennes Writers Guild.

Stacy McCandless, Joe Schwartz, John F.D. Taff, Leslee Marie Lewandowski, Chris Brannick, Justin Brock-Jones, Joe Moe, Leanne Tankel, Julia Wright, Sara Morris, Kelly Marburger, Chris Coffey, Chance Chambers, Michael Braithwaite, Stan Clyganik, Paul Mcvay, Brandon and MelSusan and Todd Theroff and everyone else who has supported me.

And special thanks to Jean DeSanto Campbell, for helping me bring out the story I wanted to tell.

"I'm very well acquainted with the seven deadly sins. I keep a busy schedule, trying to fit them in." - Warren Zevon, Mr. Bad Example

1

All I really wanted was the simple life, and a beautiful woman to share it with, but the black sheep always seemed to be having more fun on the other side of the white picket fence.

2

As I stood there watching my apartment burn, all I could think about was my brother, Joey.

Joey died the day I was born. I never even got to meet him. My grandma told me that when she and my dad took my mom to the hospital to have me, they left my brother with my Grandpa Joe. She didn't get into the gory details, but apparently Grandpa fell asleep watching television, and little Joey wandered out the front door, into the road and, more specifically, into the path of a 1979 Chevy Nova.

The driver of the car had just turned 16. I could only imagine the excitement of that first time behind the wheel alone, suddenly destroyed by obliterating a six-year old child who should never have been in the middle of the road in the first place.

Being the boy who lived left my relationship with my parents complicated. They didn't force me to live in a cupboard under the stairs or anything like that, yet my mom mistakenly called me Joey for most of my early years, when she was drunk or pilled out on antidepressants.

My mom and I were never close. I tried not to take it personal. I couldn't imagine how hard it must have been to bury one child with a newborn wanting attention. My mom was outwardly mean, and every time I would do something stupid, she would say, "I'll bet your brother wouldn't have done that."

My dad was a different type of fucked up.

He worked for UPS, but at night he would always be gone. When he was home, he would have his friends over for a game in the basement, and I don't mean pool, darts, poker or anything like that. Dad was a D &D role player. He and his friends would pretend they were knights, elves, goblins, and shit like that. He dealt with things by escaping from reality, into nerdworld.

Dad was so deep into the role-playing thing that he even went to this huge role playing convention, every year in Indianapolis. I guessed it was just a bunch of fat, smelly guys, dressed up like wizards, playing Dungeons and Dragons. I'd never been, but that's where dad met Larry.

I remember him coming home from the convention and saying he'd met this awesome guy from Indy, who played a 12th level Druid, and that the guy worked for FedEx. Mom didn't think anything about it, until dad started going back and forth to Indy more and more. Then, one night around Thanksgiving, Larry came to our house for a game.

One might think there wouldn't be any harm in a group of grown men living out their medieval fantasies in a basement, but one time mom thought everyone had left, so she went down stairs and found my old man with a mouth full of Larry. They didn't even hear her come in. Things went from weird to extremely awkward at that point, and dad left my dear mom for Druid Larry.

I didn't really have a problem with my dad leaving

my mom and me, or his lifestyle. Larry and my dad somehow managed to become the strongest example of stability in my life. The only thing I had problem with was the way he left her, because when he came out, my mother went into an even darker place with her drinking and pills. She went from being Suzy Homemaker, to Susie the Promiscuous Drunk. She stayed that way until she met my step-dad Rick.

Rick was a simple man. He like working in his garage and putting in his hours at the factory to provide for his family. He watched a lot of boxing and baseball. He drank, but not as much as my dear mom, and he eventually got her to cut it back and go to church with him and his son, Garrett.

I was forced to go to church for awhile with them, but after I fell asleep enough times, my mother and Rick were too embarrassed to take me..

They still got to parade Garrett around in his Sunday best, and talk about how great he was. He was the Stepford son my mom had always wanted. Garrett was the perfect replacement for my dead brother. He was also the perfect replacement for me, and I wasn't even dead. She still had to make room for me in her new perfectly stupid little life.

I didn't know my mom and Rick very well at all, but I didn't like them. They didn't care much for me either. Eventually, we deteriorated to only speaking on holidays.

It's kind of funny the crazy things you think about during heightened points of stress. I wasn't even concerned about all of my stuff inside the apartment. It was all the worthless shit that nobody really needs. The fire took it all, from my clothes and furniture, to my books and my record collection.

I'll bet my brother wouldn't have burned his apartment down.

3

Before the fire-

My home was an old, three story Victorian house on Williams Street. The house was divided into three apartments. The set up was weird. I had most of the top floor to myself, but my bathroom and kitchen were on the ground floor. It wasn't much, but it was a place to sleep and perpetuate my drunken existence.

It was across from empty lot. There had been a house on that lot for decades, but it burned down around the same time I moved in. The old woman that once lived across the street had lost her husband only a few days before the fire. She still liked to visit where her house had been. Sometimes she cried, and other times she threw rocks at the empty lot.

The house I lived in was falling apart, and I had heard that it was haunted, but none of that put me off as much as my two neighbors, Dan and Holly. I didn't hang out with them. They didn't even hang out together. We each stayed in our respective little shit-holes, but I always knew when they were around. I could usually hear Holly through the walls. Neither of them seemed like bad people; they were just fucking weird.

The first time I met Dan, he scared the shit out of me. He was a performing birthday party clown. It not unusual for a guy to be a clown. It was rare, but not a weird thing. It's just strange to see a clown in your front yard when you're walking to your car. I expect to see clowns at the circus or at a birthday party, but not in my day-to-day life. I was convinced someone had drugged me or that the clown had sprung from the sewers to kill me, but eventually he just became Dan.

Other than walking around in his full clown gear, Dan wasn't a bad neighbor. Without the red nose and makeup, he looked like an average, balding, overweight middle-aged man. I could have considered him a normal neighbor if it wasn't for hearing his television blaring The Three Stooges and Road Runner cartoons at all hours of the night.

Holly was a hottie. She was a pale redhead, with a schoolgirl build and bookish black-framed glasses. She wasn't that unusual by most people's standards. I might have noticed how cute she was at first, if she wasn't so goddamn annoying. She was constantly singing songs from RENT, Rocky Horror Picture Show, and Cats. The show tunes were almost as annoying as her singing a narration about everything she did. Even that wouldn't have been that bad, but she wasn't as good of a singer as she thought she was. It got to be too much sometimes.

The other annoying thing about Holly was her dog, Monk.

He was some kind of a Chihuahua/ terrier mix and Holly loved to have him sing with her. The dog had an even worse singing voice than she did, and if he wasn't yapping like a little freak in her apartment, she was in the backyard yelling for him.

A guy can only hear the word "Monk" of the phrase "Monk! Come here, boy!" so many times before he wants to murder an innocent dog in cold blood.

Monk was about the most miserable excuse for a dog that I had ever seen, but he produced some hellish piles of shit in the yard. I would have sworn that we had a German Shepherd or Labrador Retriever dropping loads in our yard, but I had seen Monk drop dookie.

I found most of his landmines with my shoes, walking into the house through the back yard, drunk.

The most comical part of the dog was that he pissed like a girl dog. He didn't lift his leg like a normal boy dog. He squatted and shook like he was going to explode. The only time he didn't squat was when the grass was wet. When it was wet outside he tried to balance on his front legs to keep his ass dry. He looked like a wobbly tripod teetering on his front legs, with his lipstick poking out.

All of my neighbors were interesting, but Monk had the most personality.

I was interested in getting to know Holly. I never bothered to talk to her too much in the beginning. My college days were long gone, and she was only in her second year. I was sure she could do better, someone more her age.

Holly the hottie didn't date much. If she did, she didn't bring many guys home. The only time I remember her bringing a guy home was right after I moved in.

I had just cracked open the new issues of Juggs magazine, when I heard her front door slam, followed by a few more slams and crashing sounds. I didn't know if I should be concerned or not. I could hear a man talking, but I couldn't hear Holly until they made it into the bedroom. They were only in the apartment for a few minutes before she started screaming like a porn star.

She was moaning, and I could hear the headboard of her bed slamming into the wall. It was hot. The magazine full of naked women in my hand, and the sounds coming from Holly's apartment were hot. I had never thought of Holly like that before that night. It was hard to think about anything but how Holly might look getting fucked stupid, her pale legs wrapped around the guy and her hair spread out on the pillow. I thought about knocking on the wall or doing something to let them know I could hear them, but instead, I did what what any good neighbor would do, I jerked off to the sounds and mental images of fucking the girl next door.

I had always had a thing for the girl next door.

4

My freshman English teacher once told me that I was a bright boy, I just wasn't willing to apply myself. I took that to heart and made sure that nobody expected anything extraordinary out of me. I had a job with Jake's Janitorial Services to make ends meet. I'm sure I was qualified to do something else with myself, but I didn't have any feeling of real self-worth. Scrubbing toilets was the perfect job for a guy with no direction towards any real future. All I had to do was clean offices two nights a week, and make the public library look presentable the other three nights of the week.

I really wasn't much more than a walking, talking cliché of a custodian, drinking to deal with my lot in life, and listening to rock music while I cleaned windows, mop floors and emptied trash. I loved the job because I just wanted to be left alone. I was left in peace with my daydreams, and, since I worked third shift, I never had to deal with real people. It was perfect, but there was something funny about it. I could clean up after other people all night; I just couldn't clean up my own shit and get my act together.

Things were fucked-up but I wasn't the kind of guy to dwell on it. I just kept on keeping on. I did what I had to do between drinks and some acceptable ladies I picked up who were kind enough to share orgasms with me. It wasn't the life for everyone but it was my life.

Being a master of the custodial arts gave me a lot of time to think. Most of the time I let my mind roam to lame movies rich with janitor quotes, like The Toxic Avenger and Earnest Scared Stupid.

I even went into work every night expecting some sort of cinematic chaos to break the monotony. It didn't happen, but I hoped one night while I was scrubbing shit off of a wall or chipping away at dried vomit on the floor, something would happen to change my life

Most of the time I was hoping against hope. In reality, I was chipping away at the days of my life while I dealt with dirty water fountains, trash, and bloody tampons. Cleaning the ladies' restrooms were the worst.

Anyone who has ever been into a ladies' restroom would know that most of them have little metal or plastic boxes mounted to the stall walls for women to stash their used tampon or pads in. They were for all of the hygiene products a girl needed to keep her box clean. That's why I called them box boxes. It's a great idea, but I didn't realize how much I had a problem with feminine hygiene products until I started cleaning public bathrooms.

At one time I loved that time of the month. I actually loved getting into a lady's business during her period. There was just something about her natural, bloodiness that got me hard. It was savage, and a little taboo. I was fantastic. I was even the kind of guy to go downtown. The clit wasn't a mess, and that was where the magic happened. I didn't mind a little blood on my fingers while I was down there, either. It wasn't like a bloody vag had any more badness. Most diseases that would be in the vag blood were in regular juices. It just made things a little more wet, and I was all for the red, wet slip-n-slide.

Those throbbing feelings were challenged after I had to start emptying the box boxes.

I found the most disgusting stuff in there. I found everything from dripping, squishy tampons and crusty toilet paper, to shitty panties and yellowish-brown pus, mixed with dried, blood-caked pads. It was gross, and there was more than a handful of times that I gagged when I opened the silver boxes, and a wave of nasty stank hit me. The whole mess made me think that I never wanted to touch another woman, ever again.

Those feeling always passed when I was in the heat of the moment, and my stank box memories faded. The smell of a real woman always brought me back.

Finding comfort with a woman was one of the many things that kept me going. I also had a regular seat at a local bar, and the ability to get lost in my music and think about better times, times when things were much simpler.

I liked to listen to the classic rock station all night, and think about the first time I heard each song or the best times I had when each song was playing. It just so happened that most of the times were in the back seat of my car or getting high with my friends. Those were the good times. The music was good, and if it wasn't, we were too high to care.

We were young, dumb, and full of cum.

My friend, Jack, had turned me onto the music I was going to love for the rest of my life. I occasionally found a new band I liked, but I just didn't get into the new rock-n-roll. It was missing something. It's possible that today's rock stars just aren't doing the right drugs.

Guns 'N' Roses and Metallica were the bands of

my generation to fuck the pooch. They ruined rock music, in my opinion. I'm sure they aren't the only ones to blame, but they led the way for groups like Nickleback. Bands like these are the reason I need to be clear when I say I dig classic rock, because I don't consider them classic rock yet.

I remember feeling like it was a dark day for music the first time I heard Metallica's overuse of vowels on classic rock radio. I thought there was something wrong with my local station. KISS and AC/DC were also not my thing. KISS was the worst. A lot of my friends liked them but I couldn't stand them. It wasn't that they were a bad band. They just made some really bad music.

Bad music was like bad people. They both were going to be around, even if I didn't want them to be, and every now and then they were going to pop up and fuck up my good time. I just had to make the best of it. I had to deal with the bad to enjoy the good.

I just wanted to enjoy some Creedance Clearwater Revival and Eric Clapton, or, God forbid, a little Warren Zevon and Bob Dylan. I wanted the people in my life to have that same level of incredible. I often just settled for the people that talked to me, especially in bars. I knew I wouldn't meet a nice girl in a bar, but finding a Dylan quality woman was next to impossible. I was lost in a sea of Nickleback bimbos and crunchy Grateful Deadheads.

Some people had church. I had the bar.

5

I didn't have just one place to drink. My favorite bars were The Speakeasy, The Pour House, The Seal Club, and The Coyote Club, but I wasn't picky. I liked almost any place that served alcohol. The trick was finding a quiet little place that served good wine.

The Speakeasy was my favorite of the three. It was the kind of place that hadn't changed much over the years. Everything had a nice layer of dust on it, and Damien Parker was the best bartender in town.

It was my favorite place to drink because Parker always kept a couple bottles of dry red wine, just for me. I still had to pay nearly the price of a bottle for one glass, but sometimes it was worth it. The only problem with The Speakeasy was that they were only open Thursday thru Saturday. That left me with the problem of finding another place to drink the rest of the week.

The Pour House was like every dive bar in the Midwest. They didn't serve wine. That meant I didn't go there unless I wanted to drink whiskey and be left alone.

My third pick was The Seal Club. It was my place

to go during the day. It always felt like night time in there. It was a dark place without windows, clocks or televisions, and it turned into a heavy metal bar during the vampire hours. I only stayed for that once, and it didn't turn out well.

The Seal Club kept wine in stock for the weirdo metalhead kids who thought they were vampires. It was a shitty budget Merlot, but those weirdos didn't care; they pretended it was blood anyway. I stomached it because I liked the gloomy atmosphere. There was just something about a dark bar that felt right.

The Coyote Club was a shitty titty bar on the edge of town. It was my least favorite place to go. Most of the dancers were train wrecks, what was left of once beautiful women. It was a dirty hole, full of perverts, but they served wine.

I tried not to get stuck in the habit of going to the same bars on the same nights of the week, but I always found myself at the Seal Club on Wednesdays. When the black leather-clad kids came in, I made my escape and started thinking about how to cap off my night. One night, when I abandoned the vampire dungeon, I didn't get very far before the glow of a late night restaurant with a bar made me consider another drink before I stumbled on home.

I drove past the front doors to see how much later they were open, but I ran up on the curb, and didn't even see the hours posted. I saw people inside enjoying adult beverages, so I steered my Chrysler into a nearby, empty parking spot. I staggered in the front door, past the frumpy-looking hostess, and into the restaurant's bar, like I hadn't been drinking for the last 4 hours.

A tanned goddess with black hair, and a B-cup that was working very hard, took my order.

She looked like a poor man's pin-up from Hot Rod calendar or a tattoo magazine. If she had had a little more meat on her bones, she would have had a nice hour-glass figure, but as it was, she had a tight little ass under her short black uniform skirt, which she twisted as she walked. I pretended not to notice.

I made small talk about drink specials. She named them off, but it was all overpriced beer and some gussied-up Long Island Iced Tea. I was a wine drinker, so I asked what wines they had. I didn't want to tell her I only had five bucks, but I had her bring me the cheapest one.

It tasted like vinegar and watered-down grape juice. Oh. well.

I hated other drunks and dumb-ass frats boys. My short fuse and low douche bag tolerance made it hard to live in a college town. These dudes were the reason I usually avoided restaurant bars. It was a good way to avoid the collection of college cretins. My usual haunts were about the only safe places to go. I hated the sports, flair and fake smiles of restaurants like Friday's and Garfield's. Their only saving grace was that they served alcohol on Sundays, but that meant being subjected to the judgmental eyes of everyone fresh from church, in their Sunday best.

The holy rollers did their best to make me feel bad about myself. I was usually looking for a little hair of the dog. They didn't know me and they looked at me like I was drinking my way to hell. I might have been, but I didn't need them to make me feel like a creep. I had the Coyote Club for that.

I felt like less of a creep in the titty bar. I knew everybody in there was some kind of creep, but I didn't go for the tits and ass. I went for the wine. They had wine as nasty as the women sliding around on the poles, but a cheap Pinot Grigio was better than nothing.

I didn't care much for the ladies at the strip club, but it was a place to drink and smoke. If I wanted to see a naked woman, I'd just rent a Marisa Tomei movie. She's naked in everything. I didn't even care about lap dances. I still got dances, but I didn't waste my money on them. Deluxury gave them to me for free. I bought her a drink sometimes, but she mostly gave me dances to avoid customers even more gnarly than I was. And she knew I wouldn't feel her up.

Deluxury, or Dee, as I called her, was a tall, bottle-blonde; a living stripper stereotype. She had a fake tan, a bad dye job, too much makeup, and an abusive ex-husband. She danced a double shift at the Coyote Club to make enough money to support her online poker habit. She reminded me of a young, white-trash Goldie Hawn.

Most of the time she just took me in the back and talked to me like I gave a shit.

She didn't really like me, she couldn't have. There really wasn't anything special about me. I wasn't in very good shape. I was average height, with average shaggy brown hair, and I had the teeth of someone who had smoked cigarettes, drunk coffee, and downed red wine for thirteen years. Of course, I had smoked cigarettes, and drunk coffee and red wine for thirteen years. I looked like I had lived the kind of life I had lived.

Dee looked like she had seen more than a few rough days, too. Years of smoking, long nights, and heavy makeup had taken a toll. She wasn't stupid. She knew it. She also knew that the men weren't looking at her face while she was on stage.

She still looked good naked, but she wasn't as sexy as the raven haired restaurant bartender in her little black skirt. The restaurant girl was a knock-out with her clothes on. It made me think about how she looked without her uniform. She was type of girl I really wanted to working her beautifully, tanned B-cup at The Coyote Club.

My naked bartender fantasies made for some very nice mental images. I let those thoughts dance around in my head, while I finished my wine. I knew the $3 glass of Merlot was the only drink I was getting before I drove back to my apartment, so I nursed it.

Soon, the other patrons filtered out into the night, and on to better things. I had heard the dark-haired girl tell another old boy that they were closing soon. I wasn't ready to leave, but I tossed back the rest of my wine, and watched everyone leave.

When they were all gone, I watched the girl bend over to count her tips and play with her cell phone. The view was nice from where I was sitting. She was sexier than any woman that would give me the time of day, but I felt like fuckin' with her anyway.

"Who's a guy gotta fuck to get a free drink around here?"

The girl didn't answer, she just brought my ticket over in a whiskey tumbler, and shot me a shitty look. The ticket said my server's name was Brittany. She looked more like a Betty or an Alexis, to me.

"I'm the only one here, but I doubt we'll be fucking tonight," she snapped.

I thought she was being a bitch, but she followed her sentence with a cocky grin that made me think I might just stand a chance with this pretty little thing. I didn't think she could really find me attractive; I was badly in need of a shave and I was nothing special. I was just an ordinary, average guy.

"So, this bad girl thing, is it just an act? It's a fashion thing, right?"

"What the fuck is that suppose to mean?"

Brittany didn't even look at me, she just kept counting.

"I'm just saying you have the dyed black hair, tattoos, and sexy, gothic, modern, pin-up girl thing going on. You must be a bad-ass, and if you are a bad girl, you wouldn't give a shit about giving away a glass a wine."

There was a long silence. She just twisted her ass in my direction while she finished fucking with her phone and counting her money. Then she jammed her tips and her phone in her purse and brought a bottle of Chardonnay over, and slammed it on the bar in front of me.

"Can you get me off?"

I pulled my last shabby five dollar bills from my front pocket, and slid them into the whiskey tumbler with my check."What do you think?"

"I think, you look experienced. Get me off and you get the bottle. You do know where a woman's clit is, right?

"As opposed to the man's clit?" I snickered, "Of course I do, but why would I eat your pussy for a bottle of wine that I can buy at the Save-A-Dime, for $3?"

Brittany gave me a shit-eating grin, and bit her bottom lip.

"Let's be honest. You don't have to, and I'm a fucking idiot for even considering it, but I just caught my fiancé cheating on me, with my sister, before I had to come work tonight," she hissed. "I've also been drinking rum all night, and I just took a hit of ecstasy, because I thought I was hooking up with my manager, who just left with some stupid bitch I can't stand."

She didn't say anything else, she just brought me another glass of wine and snatched up the dingy dollars in front of me. She didn't even count them. She just shoved all five bucks in her purse.

"Besides, you don't have three dollars, or you wouldn't be begging for a free drink."

She wiped down the bars and cleaned a few more glasses. We didn't talk. I sipped my wine and had a staring contest with a baseball report on one of the televisions, until Brittany switched them off. I didn't care. I hated baseball anyway. I just watched the blank TV.

"I gotta go get some stuff out of the back. If you want that wine, you'd better come with me. There aren't any windows back there."

I watched as Brittany walked through swinging kitchen doors, and hopped up on a table. She rubbed her hands between her legs a few time, before the doors closed. She was ready, or as ready as either of us were going to be. I was sure she felt twice as ridiculous as I did. I don't know why. I should have felt like I was winning a double, but something didn't feel right. She could have had any guy in town. I'll never know why she picked me.

I threw back the better part of the glass of wine and slid off the bar stool. I expected her to change her mind, as I walked through the cold, metal doors. She just bit her lower lip again, let out a little, nervous squeak, and spread her incredible legs.

I asked her, "Are you sure you want to do this?"

She didn't answer me again. She slipped off her expensive-looking panties and dropped them off her foot, onto the floor. I took that as a "yes," and all of that ridiculous feeling went away.

"I don't want you to feel used or objectified," I reluctantly assured her, and sighed. She pushed my head down to where my nose was even with her beautiful, shaved pussy. Of course she was clean-shaved. I usually liked a little hair down there, to remind me that I was with an adult, but she was nice, smooth and wet. She looked and she smelled the way I always imagined sexy would smell. My cock was getting hard as soon as she planted her heels into my shoulders, and my tongue met vagina.

"I'm the one using you,"she interrupted. "I'm not

going to fuck you, and I'm sure as hell not sticking your dick in my mouth. I don't know where the fuck you've been."

I thought about pretending to have some shred of dignity and self-respect. I thought about telling her to go fuck herself, but I wouldn't be fooling anyone. She was the sweetest snatch I had ever had the pleasure of tasting, and I wanted that bottle of wine.

The whole situation was pretty fucked up, but it got crazy when I started getting into my style, and I was acclimated with her body. She wouldn't let me touch her tits at first, but soon she was convulsing and carrying on like she was going to fall off of the prep table, or explode. I was almost concerned, but I had seen this reaction from women before, when I went down on them.

Soon, with her legs clamped tight around my head, I was three fingers deep into my rhythm, and discovering her nipple rings.

I could tell when she got off. At least, I was pretty sure she got off, because she screamed like an exhausted demon. She squealed and vibrated like she was having multiple orgasms, something I had actually never made happen before. Her pussy clamped around my fingers, and then she pushed me away with her foot, and sprawled out on the table.

I wiped her juices from my face on a towel from the prep area, and looked at her to confirm that she was finished. An average-sized part of me hoped she'd be so revved up that now she'd want to fuck. That was a pipe dream. There wasn't any reason she'd want to fuck me.

"Three times? I'm not even sure I've ever had a real orgasm before tonight, wow," she exhaled "three fucking times. What are you, like the magic wino orgasm fairy?"

I didn't answer her. I just walked back out to the

bar, and grabbed two bottles of their best red wine. If I wasn't getting laid, then I was going home, and getting shit-hammered.

"I think the ecstasy just kicked in," I heard her yell, as I was walking out the door.

I didn't care. Even if she wanted me to fuck her, I had already moved on and made other plans. I thought 'fuck her, fuck her relationship drama, and her perfect girl parts.'

I had wine to drink.

6

I wasn't surprised that I could get some twisty little bartender off. I wasn't any kind of sexual Jesus or anything, but I had learned how to please a woman at a young age, a mature woman. While most of my friends were losing their virginity, the only sex I was having consisted of a bottle of my mom's hand lotion and stolen issues of Penthouse. I didn't lose my virginity until my friend Jack's neighbor, Angie Cox, invited us in for a cold drink.

Jack had been mowing her yard for a couple months, and Nathan and I offered to help him one afternoon, to get it finished faster. I had never met Angie before, but my mom had always told me to stay away from her. She called her a slut and a whore. Most of the older people in the neighborhood called her the Pine Drive Prostitute. The kids at school called her Angie "Sucks Cox" or Skeletor the crack whore, because she was extremely skinny, and men were always going in and out of her trailer.

Ms. Cox wasn't an unattractive woman. Of course,

since I was 15 years old, anything with two tits, a hole and a heartbeat was fuckable, but she was probably a real looker when she was younger. Now, she just looked like she'd made a few bad choices and had a rough life.

Angie was average height, but she was so skinny that she looked like a skeleton, with tan, leathery skin hanging over bones, and a pair of perky boobs. She had a shoulder length mess of tobacco colored hair, and smoker's teeth. She also had hard lines in her face that made her look older than she was, but she had an ass like prom queen.

With all three of us mowing and weed-eating, we finished in under half an hour. We were excited, because Jack had stolen a joint from his parents, and I was going to try dope for the first time. Our plans changed when Ms. Cox invited us in. We only planned to stay a minute, but when she offered us cold beer and her own pot, a minute turned into a couple hours.

We all four passed the bong around, and I smoked more than anyone should, for their first time, but to make matters worse we were drinking beer, too.

About the time the room started spinning on me, Jack and Angie started making out, and his hands were all over her chest. They both seemed really into it. It was funny. I was so high I just watched and giggled like a nerd. Jack told me it was something they had done before, but I didn't expect them to start ripping each other's clothes off, and really didn't expect Angie to started jerking Nathan off. She just whipped his dick out and had her way with it while she was blowing Jack.

In a blur of flesh and bong smoke, she was sucking them both off. She waved me over, but I was way too stoned, and the situation was way too fucked up for my little brain. I thought I was tripping, and I was sure one of our parents was going to burst in at any moment.

I was getting a boner watching the meat triangle in

action.

Nathan was still getting a blowjob, when Angie started directing Jack. She pushed him behind her and guided his cock into her. I couldn't tell which hole she put him in, but she seemed to really like it. I sort of liked watching and Angie could tell I liked it by the trouser tent I had pitched. She waved me over again, and I started to move closer, but I was feeling the kind of paranoia only pot could produce.

Then before I could join in on the fun, and finally lose my virginity, I shot my load in my shorts. There, for anyone to see, I had prematurely gotten off, saturating my tighty-whiteys and jean shorts. It was the single, most embarrassing moment at that point of my life.

Instead of finally fucking a real woman, I ran home, covering my crotch and hid in bedroom.

Jack went on to start fucking Angie on a regular basis, like a lot of guys in town. Nathan started dating our friend Abigail. She was hot, but I pretended to not see what the fuss was all about. I was too busy trying to live down my "shoot and run" reputation. It was embarrassing, and I still didn't lose my cherry, until the day after Jack moved to Nashville to make music. Going by his house was a force of habit, but as I walked by, I saw Angie trying to wrestle four bags of groceries into her trailer.

I decided to tuck my pride between my legs and offer her a hand. She graciously accepted my help, but she had to make a crack about making sure I didn't run off, before I was finished helping. I'm sure I turned eleven shades of red, but I helped her carry in her bags anyway.

When we got inside, I noticed the reason everything was so heavy was because the majority of her groceries were cans, and most of it was canned beef ravioli and beer.

"Breakfast of Champions," I chuckled.

"A girl's got to eat, and that shit is cheap."

"At least you have all of the major food groups covered, beef and beer."

"Did you want a beer?"

"Oh, I don't think so, not after last time," I replied.

"I understand. No pressure. I was just going to have a glass of wine, would you like to try that?"

I was happy she had invited me to hang out, after our last encounter. I had always thought that wine was for women. Men drank beer and hard liquor, but most liquor tasted like spicy poison to me. I wasn't about to drink more beer with Angie and get drunk, so I took her girly wine. It was just her and me, and I needed a drink to calm my nerves.

We killed a couple bottles of Merlot that day, while we listened to Connie Francis and some other records. The more we drank, the more relaxed I felt. Then she started putting her feet on me, kissing my neck and rubbing the inside of my leg. Before I knew it, she had her head in my lap, for my first blowjob, followed by her coaching me through my first time having sex. It was uncoordinated and awkward, like a monkey trying to fuck a football, but it felt great. Afterwards, she taught me all about how to please her, and how to get most women off. She was patient and attentive. I was a good student, and I became her new boy toy.

After Nathan and Abby got married, I started going to Angie's house all the time. I didn't have anything else to do. Girls my age were busy dating assholes, and I was hooked on the whole sex, drugs, and rock 'n' roll thing.

Sometimes Angie and I would drink wine, just listen to records, and talk. Other times she'd go down on me, if I had a bad day. Sometimes I'd just go down on her, but we fucked regularly, until I started messing around with girls from my high school. Then I took everything Angie taught me, and applied it to donating orgasms to any girl nice enough to let me between her legs.

I never actually thanked Angie Cox for what she did for me. My life was changed by the wine we drank and everything we did. I learned a lot from the Pine Drive Prostitute.

She made a man out of me.

7

Ms. Cox taught me about sex, but I already knew what love was. I was the dumb-ass who fell in love with the girl next door. She was everything. She was the girl I wanted to grow up and marry, and even while I was doing stupid shit, I loved her, but I never got her.

Her name was Destiny Hinzman.

Destiny was my idea of the perfect woman. She wasn't conventionally pretty, but her light brown hair, slender nose, high cheek bones, and friendly blue eyes became the face I pictured when someone mentioned the word beautiful. Destiny was beauty.

Jack and Nathan were the only ones who knew about my stupid little crush on Destiny. They didn't tell her. They gave me a lot of shit about it, but they also did their part to get me interested in other girls, and hook me up with someone who actually wanted to date me

I had been in love with Destiny since the first grade.

I never told her, and I never got my chance with her. She had a thing for bad boys and she dated every tool in the box, from wanksters and drug dealers to guys in shitty bands and the abusive MMA types. I even imagined that she had a lesbian fling in her wilder college days. I didn't have any reason to think that. It was just something my imagination created, one lonely night with a bottle of Jerkins.

Destiny was the girl next door when I was growing up, but I wasn't one of those guys Destiny dated, unless you count the three hours we were boyfriend and girlfriend in the 8th grade, to make another boy jealous. I was always the best friend, right there with a shoulder to cry on. This cycle carried on into high school, college, and our adult lives too.

Some people might also suggest that falling in love with a girl named Destiny, I was doomed from the start, but if I wasn't, then I was sure to make sure I fucked it all up along the way. It didn't take long to be well on my way to Hell, if you believe in such things, but when I heard Destiny was getting married, I figured I had nothing to lose. I assumed I might as well make the best of it.

There is probably a special place in Hell for people who fuck bridesmaids in a church. I didn't know and I didn't care. I didn't usually bother going to church. I hadn't been in a church since one of my best friends died. It's too depressing.

I didn't want to be in a church for a wedding either. Weddings were depressing enough. They are even more fucked up when you're going to be a part of a wedding, and it goes a step further when you're going to be in the wedding of the woman you love, and you are not the groom.

Destiny looked stunning, smiling in her white dress. Watching her move around nervously, anticipating marrying another man, only reminded me of how breathtaking she could be and why I loved her. I wasn't the kind of guy to wax all poetic about things but she looked like an angel. It might be cliché but cliches are cliches for a reason, because they can illustrate a point better than a love-stricken fool could ever articulate.

Destiny and I had lost touch every now and then, but we always found each other. We had random encounters of reconnection. Like, when I moved to Indiana. She just happened to come into the video store where I worked, after she happened to move to the same city. Then when I moved to Tennessee to go to college, I found her in my COMP 1 class. It just happened.

Over the years I got into drugs, drinking, sex and other family values. I had become the hard fucking, chain-smoking bad boy Destiny went for. That was around the same time she found God. It was all around the same time she found Elmer.

Elmer Dumas, or dumb-ass as I liked to call him, was also the guy that helped her find God and get away from the bad-boy types. He was a backwards redneck, but I was already ballsdeep in bad choices. There was no turning back to being the good guy, and that meant Elmer dumb-ass got the girl. I thought he was an asshole. I wanted her to be happy, but I hated him.

So, now I was pigeon-holed into the best friend role for the rest of my life, and that meant I was doomed to be a part of her wedding to another man. She even wanted me to be her Man of Honor, but "some people" thought it was too weird. I thought being demoted might have gotten me out of the torture of being in the wedding at all, but Destiny somehow convinced Elmer to have me as a groomsman, so I could be a part of their special day.

I would much rather have set him on fire with their unity candle, but I agreed. I did it for Destiny, that and the open bar. I hated weddings but I loved receptions. It was the best place to meet single bridesmaids. It was my lot in life. Some simpleton got the girl I loved, and I got the bridesmaid.

Always the bridesmaid, never the bride.

The particular bridesmaid at this wedding was a girl named Margie, or Marcy. I didn't actually catch her name, and she didn't bother to waste much time with pleasantries. She made her ugly dress look pretty fucking fantastic, but I thought it looked even better on the floor of the storage room.

After Destiny's mom introduced us, I offered her a nip of whiskey and she took it like a champ. "Damn, don't kill it. That has to last until we get to the reception."

"Thanks, I needed that, but aren't you worried about getting drunk in a church?"

"I just brought enough to take the edge off. I hate this shit."

"Maybe I can make it up to you."

"Nice try, but they already told me the bar was an open bar. You can't offer to buy me a drink."

"I wasn't talking about getting you a drink. I was talking about helping you take the edge off."

"I'll bite. What are you getting at?"

"Come on, Harlow. I'm the only girl in the wedding party besides the bride that you haven't slept with, and from what I hear, I'm missing out."

"I'm not sure that's entirely true. I don't remember the other bridesmaids and I don't think I actually fucked the maid of honor. She just gave me a blowjob a couple years ago."

"Sara, the maid of honor, remembers it a little differently, and I hear that you actually know Tina, the other bridesmaid very well, but that was before she lost the weight, hit the tanning bed, and bleached her hair."

"I didn't even recognize either one of them. My, how they've grown since college."

"They married into money, and now they're the Real Housewives of some stupid little farm town nobody has ever heard of."

"How sad for them."

"I don't really care about them. I'm curious about if you are as willing to defile a bridesmaid in a church as you are to cuss and drink."

"I'd be lying if I said that you didn't make your ugly dress look pretty good. Are you wearing panties with that thing?"

"I was. I'm not now."

I didn't understand how we had tumbled into this conversation. I wasn't a pretty guy. I was cute like a dirty, stray dog at best. I knew how to please a woman, but I didn't think I was anything special, and I sure as hell didn't think I had any ability to leave a lasting memory on any woman.

A few minutes later we were in the storage room, her dress hit the floor, and I was jack-hammering away at her on a table in the corner. I was pretty sure under normal circumstances that she would have been a screamer, but she had her hands cupped over her mouth to muffle the sound. I was pretty sure that the noises were going to give us away, but I wasn't going to stop until I was finished. It was fine if she got hers. I knew she really wasn't Destiny, but for all intents and purposes she was the next best thing, and with my sunglasses on, her copper-toned tresses looked more like Destiny's mousey brown colored hair.

I could hear people in the hall looking for both of us. They were talking about not being able to start without us and I wasn't going to fuck up Destiny's wedding to bang her stand in. I was actually about to stop when I got off.

I was pretty sure Margret got off. She wasn't very tight at all, but she was incredibly sensitive. She jerked and convulsed like I was electrocuting her. It felt good, but it was hard to get a grove and seal the deal. When I finished, I had to stagger back and collect myself. My legs were tender and I was in serious need of a tasty beverage.

My flask was nearly empty but it had enough to get my whistle wet and offer Marcy a swig.

Maggie had collapsed exhausted on the table. "I think that might have been worth eternal damnation."

"That's one option."

I pulled my pants up, put my jacket back on, and grabbed a cigarette from the inside pocket. I knew people were already looking for us. I only hoped I could sneak in a couple drags before the ceremony began.

"We should do that again later," Marlene said, while she recomposed herself.

I didn't reply or wait for her to get ready. I shoved a cigarette in my mouth and walked out of the room. Margie's getting her shit together would undoubtedly give me enough time to smoke, but my hasty retreat was hindered by a nervous little man-child, named Gil.

Gil was Elmer's best man. He was the only guy who could make Elmer look cool by comparison. There was no way I could ever take him seriously. He looked like a combination of a pig and Rob Schneider, if Rob Schneider was a bald pedophile.

"Where have you been? I've looked everywhere," he said. "It's time to start!"

"Relax! We're still waiting on Maxine."

"You mean Margie?"

"Whatever."

I shrugged and moved towards the front door. Gil stepped in front of me like he thought he could stop me. I put my unlit cigarette between my lips and he still didn't move, so I shoved my empty flask down the front of his pants, to hide any evidence of wrongdoing, and walked out to have a smoke.

Gil just stood there. I wasn't worried about him

saying anything to Destiny. I took him for the kind of guy who would say shit if he had a mouth full. He almost seemed amused with my antics. He only shook his head in disbelief when Margie came out of the storage room adjusting her dress.

When the wedding ceremony began, nobody bothered to tell me that only half of my shirttail was tucked in. I also didn't notice I was still wearing my sunglasses until the preacher asked Destiny the required questions. I think she was trying to subtly point out that I had been wearing my sunglasses through most of the ceremony because she was giving me a weird look until the preacher asked her if she "takes this man..."

At that point, I smiled at Destiny and tucked the sunglasses into my inside jacket pocket.

While I was smiling at Destiny, she returned her attention to her future husband. That was when I noticed Margie smiling at me and biting her bottom lip like a horny school girl. Her lustful attention brought me back to the real world, and my true place in the whole mess.

I shot her a cocky grin and put my sunglasses back on.

After the horrible ritual sacrifice was over, the wedding party was told to line up in the foyer of the church. I was told that we had to shake hands and give hugs to people as they left. I was sure I deserved that cruel and unusual punishment for any one of the many things I had done wrong in my life, but I opted to duck out.

I tried to walk past the group and Margie grabbed my arm. "We're supposed to stand here and thank people for coming."

I pulled arm away. "You have fun with that, and tell me how it goes."

Destiny gave me a look of disapproval but it turned into a smile, when I gave her the sad puppy eyes.

"I needs a smoke," I said sneaking in to give Destiny a hug and a kiss on the cheek. "It's a nasty habit but someone has to do it, right?"

"I'm so happy you're here," Destiny said

"I doubt that," I replied.

"No, I'm serious. It really means a lot to me. I know this is really not the sort of thing you enjoy."

"You don't know the half of it."

"If it makes you feel any better, we have an open bar at the reception."

"That actually does make me feel a little better."

"Destiny insisted we have an open bar," Elmer interrupted. "I'm sure she had you in mind."

"What can I say? I love my vices and I try to be on her mind every chance I get."

"It means a lot to my wife that you are here today."

"Yeah. Well," I scoffed, "I'm gonna do that smoking thing. I hear they'll kill me if I keep it up."

I held up my unlit cigarette with one hand and slapped Elmer on the shoulder with the other.

"You're a lucky guy, dumb-ass!"

My sudden movement made him flinch like he thought I was going to knock him out. It made Margie chuckle, but I didn't have any intention of hitting him. I didn't assume it would have won me any points with Destiny and I wasn't a total savage. It would take a real prick to punch someone in goddamn church. I went outside and lit my cigarette.

Destiny and Elmer looked so fucking happy shaking hands, and hugging everyone as they made their way outside. It had a nasty affect on my acid reflux. I don't even know why I kept watching. I could have moved to smoke my cigarette. I was probably in the way and I pretended not to notice, but in reality I just didn't care. I just exhaled my toxic little cloud, causing people to wave smoke out of their face and cough as they walked past.

Then it was time to throw rice and celebrate, as the bride and pudgy groom walked out of the church. Everyone cheered as they exited the church. The peasants rejoiced and passed on generic congratulations. I wasn't one of the peasants. I didn't feel like rejoicing. I felt like getting to the reception and I felt like drinking to forget.

At the reception I helped myself to all of the free wine I could get my hands on, while I watched Destiny and her friends dancing. I just wanted to watch and drink, but some people had other ideas. I wasn't a dancer but I might have joined them if Destiny invited me. Instead, Margie was dancing like a little temptress. She kept gesturing for me to join them but I waved her off once.

The second time she actually came over to the table to try to pull me to the floor. "Come on!" she begged, "The real party's on the dance floor!"

"No thanks. Harlow Don't Dance."

"Please, I wanna dance with you! Come on!"

"I said no."

"We walked down the aisle together. The least you could do is dance with me. Pretty please me with my cherry on top?!

"What? What the fuck? No! Fuck off!"

I may have come off a little too harsh but when some stupid club song started she forgot about me for a moment.

"I love this song," she squealed on her way back to the dance floor.

She ignored me while she danced with Destiny and the other girls, but soon she turned her attention to me again. I barely noticed. I was watching Destiny. I just happened to catch Margie giving me a pouty face out of the corner of my eye. She did the little playful come hither finger gesture and I finally gave her a finger gesture of my own. Flipping her off was the one thing that finally made her ignore me. It thoroughly pissed her off, and I was finally able to get back to my alcohol poisoning in peace.

Everything was cool until it was time for the $1 dances with the bride.

I wasn't drunk but I had enough booze in my system to lower my inhibitions. It was the blessing and the curse of having a high tolerance. I didn't want to watch anyone dance with Destiny. I didn't want to have to watch her get married either, but if I was going to play sort of nice, I wanted to do it drunk.

Since I wasn't yet good and drunk enough, and the opportunity presented itself, I decided to take my dollar and my lowered inhibitions to the danced floor.

I waited for the best man to finish his dance with Destiny, but I ignored everyone else in line. I also ignored the whole idea of social niceties and cut in and hogged the bride for an entire song.

"What are you doing?"

"Don't worry I'll pay for my dance but I think you're worth a whole hell of a lot than a dollar. These fucks don't even deserve a dance with you."

"You're drunk."

"Am not, but if you give me a little more time, I'll be on cloud nine and everything will be fine. We lesser men drink our pain away."

"I don't understand. Is there something you'd like to get off of your chest, Harlow?"

"No, forget it."

I tried to be all cool about everything, but that was when the last drink hit me and I decided to let it out. It was already too late but I didn't know if I would ever have another chance. I had to tell her how I felt.

"Actually, yeah," I said. "I have been in love with

you since the 3rd grade, Destiny. You are the reason I am who I am today!

"I'm the reason you're a socially awkward, promiscuous alcoholic?"

"Sorta. Let me finish."

"The song's over"

"Please, let me finish."

"Fine. Continue."

"I stood by you for all of those colossal fuck-tards you dated. I was there for you when that Paul guy convinced you to have sex for the first time and you weren't ready. I was also there when that other douche-bag dumped you because you wouldn't give him head in the guys' locker room. I even beat the shit out of your prom date when you caught him fingering Leanne in your car."

The music was over but nobody cleared off the dance floor, and the DJ didn't start another song. Everyone gawked at us while I unburdened my heart, to tell Destiny everything. I knew nothing could come of it, but I had to get it out. I had to let her know how I felt and I didn't care how it made me look. I didn't care what her new husband or anyone at the reception thought. It needed to be out there.

She started to cry. "Is there anything else?"

"Yes. I did all that. That guy even came back with his friends and kicked my ass, but I never told you that. I didn't want you to feel guilty or responsible in any way. I've never wanted you to feel anything, but happy AND sweet Jebus, maybe a little reciprocation of the love I have for you!"

There were a few moments of silence. Destiny went from looking hurt, to looking like I had thoroughly pissed her off. She had the angry look for a while before she finally smiled at me and told me what was on her mind.

"I do love you, but I grew to love you like a brother or the way you love a best friend," Destiny replied. "You always dated dumb, slutty girls. I thought that was the sort of girl you were into."

"Ya take what you can get, right?"

"You said your piece now, please, let me finish,' she said. "You were always there for me and in a crazy kind of way you mean more to me than any man in my life, but then you became the kind of guy I swore I'd never date again. Then I met Elmer. He was different."

"You do love me then, huh?"

"Of course I do, but not like the kind of love you think you're looking for and you clearly need. It's not the kind of love where you will ever see me naked."

"As much as that sucks, at least we got all of that out in the open, but to be honest, I've already come to terms with you never being mine."

I didn't wait for her to say anything else. There wasn't anything else to be said. The only thing I could do was walk away and try to save what little bit of pride I had left. I walked away and I thought about walking out the door. I should have but in a fit of masochistic glory I stayed.

I may have been a jerk but I wasn't going to be the kind of jerk to walk out on the woman I loved on her wedding day. It might have been smarter to leave but making good choices wasn't my style. I decided to stay and try to get drunker instead.

The wine was finally starting to do the trick when Gil sat down at my table. "Ya know, I had serious intentions of trying to hook up with Margie, but you kinda screwed that up for me."

"You could still make a run at her. I think your chances are pretty good. There's nothing serious between me and her. I think I might have even pissed her off."

"Yeah," Gil said, "You've pissed off a lot of people

today."

"I have a habit of doing that in public places. I hope you can find it in your heart to forgive me, if not, that's cool too."

"I didn't stand a chance with Margie anyway."

"Don't sell yourself short. She doesn't seem to be full of morals, standards or scruples of any kind. I think you have a pretty good shot."

Gil and I sat, not talking, for a long while. I spent most of the time wishing Destiny would come to her senses, run over to me and drag me out the church door, so we could start our wild and crazy life together, but I knew it wasn't going to happen. I spent the rest of the time wishing Gil would just go away.

He had apparently been talking to me the whole time, but I didn't hear him until he asked me a very honest question. "Other than Destiny, what did you always want to do before you died?"

I had spent so much time screwing things up while I waited for Destiny that I hadn't really ever thought about it. "I don't know.

Gil's question made me think, and the more I was thinking, the more I was drinking.

We talked about his failed marriage and all of the women he never took a chance on. I told him all of the stories about Destiny and me. I told him about holding out for her, and becoming the guy I thought she wanted. It was weird talking to him about the whole thing, since he was Elmer's friend.

I made sure to give him hell about that too.

We talked until I had to piss too bad to hold it anymore. I was about to excuse myself, but as I stood up the room started spinning. I steadied myself enough to make it to the bathroom but I didn't remember the walk there. I only remember a sea of semi-familiar faces asking me if I was alright.

"I need to piss," I slurred.

I recall Gil helping me to the restroom but he didn't go in with me. That would have been too weird. He waited outside and I leaned my head again the wall, while I positioned myself at the urinal, next to another familiar face.

I looked at the guy next to me but I couldn't remember who he was or how I knew him. He was a well groomed man, several years older than me. I thought it was Destiny's dad but I wasn't sure. He could have been an uncle or even a teacher from high school too. It could have even been the preacher for all I knew.

He was nice enough. He scooted over to give me my space and to avoid my back-splash. I wasn't concerned with pissing on myself. I was too busy gawking at the guy, trying to remember where I knew him from. It wasn't my proudest moment. A man should never stare at another man at a urinal, with his dick in his hand.

The guy took it well though. He knew I was wasted. He just laughed at me, finished his business, put his unit away.

"Nice cock, very professional," he said, as he washed his hands.

By the time I figured out what he said he was already out the door. I thought I must have heard him wrong, but even in my inebriated state there was no mistaking what he said. He spoke clearly and his words baffled me. Nobody had ever told me that. I had sure as hell had never had my cock complimented in a public restroom before, let alone in a church. It felt slightly dirty.

I was done pissing but I was still standing there with my dick in my hand. I wasn't sure if should be proud or violated. It didn't even matter because while I pondered the man's words my knees decided they were too drunk to support me, causing me to crumple to the bathroom floor, bashing my face on the urinal on the way down.

Things got really blurry at that point.

Gil came in to check on me and started freaking out when he saw my busted nose.

I grabbed the beer out of his hand and greeted him with the best smile I could produce. "Welcome to my humble commode!"

I didn't realize it then but in that moment, not my finest moment, my dick was still hanging out of my pants. I was busted and bloody and drunk as a wino skunk. I was pathetic, even for me. The worst part was when people started crowding into the bathroom to see what was going on.

I felt a hand tuck my junk back in my pants and I was ready to get defensive. I assumed it was Gil trying to help a guy out but it was a woman's hand. I didn't recognize the hand but I knew her face. It was a woman that had saved my ass more than once but a woman I had never dared to bed.

Her name was Alice, and if Destiny was the queen of cool, Alice was a contender for the throne. In a way, she was even more amazing, because, while I loved Destiny with all of my heart, and I swore to wait for her for the rest of my life, I always thought Alice was too cool for me.

I sort of thought one day Destiny would come around and we would live happily ever after, but I didn't think I even stood a chance with Alice. I thought so little of my chances I never even tried with her.

Alice was an artist with incredible taste in music. She dated my friend Jack for a little bit in high school but they broke up over an argument about the Beatles and the Rolling Stones. She eventually got away from it all and landed herself in art school. After that she was an enigma. A short, spitfire, raven-haired enigma with lovely lady lumps. She was a sexy hellcat with the face of an "Angel."

"No. I'm Alice," she said. "You don't remember?"

Of course. I was just thinking aloud.

"Did I say all of that?"

"We can talk later. You're drunk and we need to get you home."

"I can drive him," Gil offered

Before Alice could agree, I interjected, "No! I just met you and I thought you touched my penis!"

Everyone in the bathroom laughed, and I noticed that the crowd had a lot of familiar faces. I saw my old friend Nathan, Margie the bridesmaid, Destiny's mom, the man who said I had a very professional penis, Elmer, a couple people I didn't know and there was also Gil and Alice.

"I'm the one who touched your penis, Harlow," Alice laughed. "Don't act like it wasn't good for you. I just tucked it back in your pants. Calm down. You don't want everyone to see that thing do you?"

Elmer spoke up before I got the chance. "He might as well. He's already shown his ass."

I tried to shoot back at the groom but my words were stifled and my eyes couldn't focus. I was spinning and I wanted to see if Destiny was a face in the crowd. I didn't see her but I wanted her to be there. I wanted her there but I didn't want her to see me in such a state.

"I want him out of here and out of my wedding reception," Elmer yelled. "He has caused enough drama for one night."

"Take it easy. The guy's a mess right now. He needs help," Gil said.

"Screw you, Gil. Don't stick up for that piece of crap."

"Easy, brother! I'm just saying, go enjoy yourself.

We'll take care of this. Everyone go enjoy the reception."

"Go ahead and take care of your new buddy, but I want him gone. I'll enjoy my reception when he's out of here and out of my life."

I wanted to thank Gil for sticking up for me but every time I opened my mouth to talk I felt like throwing up. I tried to keep my mouth shut. He and Alice were helping me to a car, and puking on the people who were trying to help you was bad no matter what.

The cool night air felt good and the ice on my nose felt even better.

Somehow Alice convinced Gil to let her take me home. I was lucky they were there. I was concentrating on my not throwing up on them, and I couldn't help but think I might have gotten my ass kicked if they hadn't been there for me.

I was counting those blessing prematurely, when Elmer appeared outside and dragged me out of Alice's car.

"You've insulted me, you screwed half the wedding party in the church, made a total ass of yourself by fucking up my wedding, and said things to my wife I can't let go. I want you stay away from her and stay out of our lives forever, you diseased, faggot prick!"

I was about to say something very witty in response when Elmer swung and hit me in the gut. The punch doubled me over, putting my face at Elmer's crotch level. Words were forced aside as a rush of stomach acid, wine and once-eaten finger foods spewed all over his pants and shoes. He jumped back and cocked his fists to swing at me again, but Destiny stepped between us.

I was able to talk again after I finished puking."I hope those were rentals, asshole!"

"Stop it, both of you," Destiny screamed. "This is my wedding day, and I will not have it end like this!"

I couldn't tell if she was pissed, and she had tears in her eyes.

Seeing her cry was one of the worst things in the world to me. It made me feel like a complete fuck-up. I was usually the one to console her when she cried but our roles had changed. Elmer would be the one to console her now. Everything changed for me at that point.

"Elmer, I want you to go back inside and get cleaned up."

"I'm not going-" he started to protest.

"I don't care. Go inside and I'll make sure Harlow leaves."

Elmer didn't say anything else. He huffed back inside. Everyone went back in except Destiny, Alice, and Gil.

"I don't even know what to say to you right now, Harlow," said Destiny, "you are my best friend, and you've fucked up my wedding day, puked on my husband, and destroyed any chance of a normal friendship between us all in one night. I think you need to leave before you set fire to anything or rape my mom or something."

"Destiny, I'm so-"

"Save it. You are a fucking mess. I don't even know this person you are right now, but I know there is no way I could ever love him. Sort your shit out and find a way back into my life."

She pulled me in for a hug. It was a nice warm hug, and she smelled delicious. She had ripped me a new asshole but she was still my ideal woman. I didn't really know how to respond. She had never been so cold to me before. She was right, but I knew I was past the point of no return. I knew she didn't need me like I was.

I leaned close to her ear, careful not to get my puke breath in her face and said, "If I ever fall in love with another woman, I will make sure that she's just like you," or something like that.

8

When Alice and I left the wedding, I passed out. I must have woken at some point and walked into the hotel, but the room I walked into wasn't my own. Alice took me back to her hotel room.

Destiny and Elmer had been nice enough to rent all of the out of town guest and wedding party members cheap motel rooms. The rooms were at a little local motel, a mile or two from the church. It wasn't much, but bitching about a free motel room was low, even for me.

All of the rooms looked the same, but I figured out that I woke up in Alice's bed. I was wearing nothing but my boxers, and a bandage on my nose. Her sheets were caked with dried blood and a little puke, but she wasn't in the bed with me. I assumed she was in the shower. I could hear the shower running, and I thought about joining her, but I wasn't nearly brave enough. I was beaten up enough, and I was mildly afraid that she had dumped me in Gil's room. The last thing I needed was to hop in the shower with that guy. He might like it.

I was happy to see it was Alice who walked out of the bathroom when the shower stopped. It hurt to smile, and I couldn't see her very well with my hung-over eyes, but I think she made the little white motel towel look good.

She poured some coffee from the motel pot, and sat it next to the bed. "I didn't know what room you were in. It only seemed right to let you crash here, and I didn't want to just leave you in my car."

"That's very sweet of you. I'm curious though. Did we?"

"I don't know what makes you think I'm that kind of girl, but, no, we didn't," Alice laughed. "You were a dead man walking. You passed out right after we left the reception. I woke you up when we got here, and you walked like a zombie from the car. I don't even think you were awake."

"You can't blame a guy for wishful thinking."

"Wishful thinking? Last night you told Destiny you loved her on the dance floor at her wedding and the next morning you're going to tell me that you wish we would have did the dirty?"

"I'm sorry. It's a compliment. I just assumed that since I was practically naked in your bed that I had messed up your sheets with some good bodily fluids too."

"That's disgusting. No. You only bled all over them, and the puke was on your shirt when you flopped down. You were nice enough to take your pants and everything else off at the front door, leaving me a trail of nasty clothes. Thanks for that."

"Why am I in your bed then?"

Alice sat on the bed, careful not to let her towel fall. "That's easy. You're an asshole."

"I am a real jerk, aren't I?"

"Yeah, in more ways than one."

"Why'd you help me if I'm such a jerk?"

"I don't know. It seemed like the thing to do," she smiled. "You're a jerk but I didn't want to just leave you for dead."

"Sometimes I think that's my lot in life. Maybe that's where I should be."

"That sounds pretty pathetic. I think you and I both know that you have more worth than that. What are doing with yourself?"

"I do a lot of drinking and getting myself into just enough trouble to keep life interesting. I guess I'm not really doing anything worth a shit with my life."

"Geez, as much as a woman loves to have sex with a guy full of depression issues and zero direction, I think perhaps I need to get you back to your car. You should get a shower. You kind of smell like a corpse."

"Shot down just like that, huh?"

"Shot down? Harlow, I haven't seen you in years. You are still holding a giant torch for Destiny. I don't have time to adopt a man and fix him up, and I'm not the kind of woman who fucks a guy, just because he's devilishly handsome and kinda charming. We're not getting any younger. I'm looking for the real deal."

"But," I smiled, "You do think I'm charming and handsome?"

"I said devilishly handsome. I won't deny that, but you need to get yourself together. If you can do that, then you can call me. I think you have all of the potential in the world to be a great guy."

"I've heard that my whole life. Everyone says that I have so much potential, I just don't apply myself."

"Maybe you need to apply yourself for a change. Maybe you just need to stop dwelling on Destiny. She's a married woman now. You need to focus on you, and work your stuff out. Then we can talk about how incredible the sex would be with us."

"Oh! You are such a tease!"

"Call it incentive to get your act together. Now get in the shower." She pointed to the bathroom.

While I let the water rinse over me, washing the stink and humility of the preceding day's event's off of me, I thought about what Alice had said. In a funny way, she had basically told me that I did stand a chance with her. The only thing in my way was my obsession with Destiny and my self-destructive bullshit. My tunnel vision had me locked on Destiny and the pipe dream that she might one day be interested in me. I was so locked in on that one thing, that I never even considered that I might have a chance with Alice.

I knew that she had given me a deep reality check. She had cut off my balls and humbled me with her words of wisdom. In one comment, she pointed out all of my flaws. She did it with a samurai-like accuracy. I wasn't sure where such brutal honesty had come from, but she nailed me like she knew me or at least knew about me.

It made me think that she might have asked about me, and that was all I needed to know. I knew that I had been codependent to the idea of Destiny coming around, and me trying to be the guy I thought she wanted me to be. Knowing this made me think how easy it would be to turn it around, to be the guy Alice saw in me. I was delusional enough to think that I cared enough about myself to make the switch, and suddenly I was willing to get my shit together for Alice, and to maybe at least have a chance at re-establishing my friendship with Destiny.

After my shower I was so refreshed and so clean, with a fresh look on a lot of things.

When Alice dropped me off at my car, she handed me a piece of paper with her number on it. "I'm going to New York for a couple months. Then I'll be in Chicago for a bit. I really hope things get better for you."

"Thanks. I hope you have safe travels. I'd like to see you again, maybe under different circumstances."

"That might be nice."

"It would be incredible. I think we have a lot of stuff to talk about, if you're interested. I have a lot to say on the matter of crushes, projecting the wrong image, and making a shit-ton of bad choices."

Alice just rolled her eyes."I think I read that book."

"I'm serious. You've made me do a lot of thinking."

"It's only been a couple hours."

"I was thinking about applying that potential."

"I think that sounds nice, but it's not going to be as easy as it might have seemed while you were jerking off in the shower and thinking about it."

"There was no jerking off, I promise. Sometimes I even surprise myself," I said. "Historically, I would have defiled you in a shower fantasy, but I was too busy thinking about everything you said."

"That's very sweet. I don't think a guy has ever told me that he wanted to defile me in a shower fantasy before."

"I doubt that."

"I'm sure it's happened. I'm not stupid. I talk to men every day. A few of them, or one of my ex boyfriends might have whacked-off to mental images of me before. I'm not conceited enough to assume that as a fact, but I've never had anybody crass enough to tell me they'd actually do it."

"I'm sorry. I'm trying to give you a compliment. Was that too much?"

"It's fine. I like you, Harlow, but we have a ways before we cross that bridge."

"I understand that but I really would like to get together, in the near future. I would love to just talk."

"Just talk?"

"Yes, just talk. I have my shower time until then. You might be interested in my story of a girl I knew, that I thought was too cool to approach."

"We'll see how serious you are. You have my cell number."

"I think I like that. I have a lot to think about."

Alice leaned toward me with a big smile on her face. "I'll give you something else to think about."

She pulled me in for a hug. I obliged and took in her warm vanilla scent. I could feel her chest against mine. The compress of her body and the scent of her gave me half a chub. I tried to make sure she didn't notice, but she gave me a clever little smile. I smiled back and pressed her mouth against mine. She kissed me so hard I could taste blood. My lips dug into my teeth and she pulled my bottom lip between hers and ran her tongue the length of it. She ended the contact with a few more passionate passes, kissing me deeper each time, pulling away with that smile on her face

"I hope you call, but don't waste my time, Harlow."

I didn't know what to say, so I just brushed her hair out of her eyes with my hand, gave her a nervous smile and got out of her car. I was feeling incredible. I felt like I had a plan. It wasn't a solid plan, or a sure thing, but I had the possible chance to both have my best friend back, and an incredible opportunity with the woman that I thought was too cool for me.

All I had to do was get my act together. I had a lot to think about. I didn't know what I wanted to do with myself, and I couldn't stop thinking about what Alice said. I also kept bouncing back to the question Gil asked me about what I wanted to do with my life. I didn't have any idea.

Instead of going home I decided to get a bottle of wine, and drive to Oak Hills to see my other best friend, Jack.

9

I met Jack MacManus the summer before I was about to go into high school, and he introduced me to my other good friend, Nathan Zimmerman. They were both a year a head of me, but they seemed even older than that. Jack loved music but he also loved the ladies. He and Nathan were always talking about great bands, how drunk they got, and how much pussy they were going to get.

I thought they were the kings of cool, and overnight I had gone from a Dungeons and Dragons dice throwing metal head, to pussy hunting, beer drinking dude. I didn't have any choice. I put the comics down and started drinking and swiping titty magazines from the newsstand by my house.

After I barely graduated high school, I had moved to Nashville to live with Jack. He was my best friend, and I needed to get the hell out of the small town life for a while. I needed to make a life for myself and figure out what I wanted to do.

I might have also heard that Destiny was going to school in Nashville.

Nathan and Abigail got married and moved up around Chicago. He wanted to get out of the small Midwest tow life. We still saw him and Abby every now and then, but he grew apart from Jack and me. It could also be said that he grew up.

My place was with Jack. He was the friend that got me into music. We were closer than Nathan and me. I really only knew Nathan through Jack. Jack was a real people person like that. He got along with everyone. He was always introducing me to new people, but music was his thing.

While most kids played cowboys and Indians or superheroes, Jack listened to and admired Bob Dylan, John Lennon, Joey Ramone, and, much later, Lou Reed, Tom Waits, Nick Cave, and Kurt Cobain. Thanks in part to his heroes, Jack became one of the best song writers I have ever heard. He even taught himself guitar at the age of 13, and had learned drums by 17. Jack could also pick up and play almost any other instrument by ear.

To know Jack was to love him. He was so passionate about music, it became infectious to everyone around him. He lived for it. Jack was happy as long as he had his guitar, a few good friends, and a place to rest his head at night. Some people think it was Jack's peace-loving, easy-to-get-along-with attitude that allowed him to fall into drugs. To Jack, and to many others, --sex, drugs and rock'n'roll went hand in hand in hand.

He was a fountain of music and knowledge, with a child-like enthusiasm for life. It didn't matter if you were a jock, a hippie, a motor-head, or a punk, Jack was the guy everyone wanted at their parties. Being friends with him meant I got invited too.

He had a huge record collection, that came mostly from yard sales and from obscure music stores, most of which were no longer around. People would also give him records all the time, just because. I remember how excited I was the day I found him a copy of the *Rock 'n' Roll High School* soundtrack on vinyl. I had never given him a record before, and I wanted it to be the first. He already had a copy, but he traded me a copy of Johnny Cash *Live From Folsom Prison*. That album would become my all time favorite.

People jokingly called Jack "the resident alcoholic", not that alcoholism is anything to joke about, but we all loved to watch him get shit-hammered and tell his stories about the time he met Iggy Pop or how Bob Dylan was the best artist of all time. He would talk for hours and we'd all listen as long as he talked.

One of the cool things about Jack was that he was into making mix tapes, and those tapes changed lives. I remember the morning my neighbor, Chris Hardman, missed the bus, and Jack agreed to give him a ride to school. Jack had made a mix tape of songs that included a slew of KISS b-sides. Chris had heard the KISS classics like 'Beth', but once he heard their other stuff, he was forever altered.

Jack taught Chris how to play the drums like Peter "The Cat" Criss, and hooked him up with tapes of every KISS song ever recorded. Soon, Chris changed his name to Kriss, and went from being a bible thumping, bully bull's-eye to being the Doctor of Love!

Jack turned almost everyone in our high school onto their favorite bands. Something I sure most of them never appreciated the same way I did, but he didn't just turn me onto one of my favorite bands, he turned me onto all of them. He opened my eyes to a whole new world and way of thinking.

The only problem was, the more time I spent with Jack, I noticed that his drug and alcohol abuse was becoming more than just something fun to do at parties. We did drugs because the rock stars we loved did drugs. It had started with drinking and smoking pot for fun, but it turned into a cycle where we couldn't do anything unless we were drunk or high. It was becoming a serious problem.

Jack started smoking pot alone to "help him sleep," and then he just snorted a fat line of coke when it was time to get up. One line turned into two, turned into three. Before long, I couldn't even keep up with all of the drugs he was into.

He convinced me to try pot, mushrooms, and cocaine, but I drew the line at heroin and the other stuff.

I had run into Destiny at a bar, during the time I was living with Jack, and after we reconnected, she helped me get back into school. I was only taking general study classes but I didn't want to screw it up, mostly because I didn't want Destiny to be disappointed in me. I was already fighting to stay in college and actually leave with some kind of degree, but Jack didn't have school or any responsibility to speak of. All he had to do was get fucked up and play a show in some bar or two, for enough money to cover his part of the rent.

People gave Jack drugs like they gave him records, when we were kids. He'd stay up for six or seven days in a row, followed by six to seven days of just sleeping. It became pretty pathetic. He became pretty pathetic.

I didn't get involved when his girlfriend dumped him, because he picked the drugs over her. I didn't say anything when he was too fucked-up to care blowing off a meeting with a guy from a major record label. I didn't feel like fucking up my happiness to babysit him.

I stayed anywhere to avoid his shit. I spent most of my time with the girl I was dating. I was pretty happy. I just minded my own business until the day I got a call from his ex-girlfriend, Kelly. She said that Jack had overdosed on methadone and was in the hospital, on suicide watch.

Jack was still asleep when I came into his hospital

room. I didn't want to wake him up, so I just sat there and tried to figure out what I was going to say when he opened his eyes. I had made up my mind during the drive that I was going to lay down the law to Jack, once and for all.

He was either going to get clean or I was finished with him. I had a rough outline of my lecture, when my phone rang.

I darted into the hallway to take the call, and to my surprise it was my cousin, Gavin Bennett, the same guy Jack had blown a deal with less than a year earlier. He was looking to borrow some money again, and it got the wheels in my head turning. This could be my chance to help everyone.

After a lengthy conversation I convinced Gavin to meet with Jack again, if I gave Gavin the money he needed. In return Jack was going to have to stay clean and sober for at least a year before he could sign any record deal. Getting to see my friend live and get sober was worth the money to me.

Jack was already sitting up in the bed when I walked back into the room. He had heard the entire conversation. I was a little afraid he was going to be pissed at me, but it was worth the risk.

"Make it three years sober, and we all have a deal." he said with a nervous smile.

I called Gavin back, and he agreed to the deal because he would be the only one getting what they wanted instantly. Jack and I were both going to have to wait three whole years to have what we wanted. Three years sounded like a really long time but if Jack made a record, I'd get to see my best friend happy. I had faith in him.

There were some extremely rough nights, and Jack took up smoking regular cigarettes for the first time in his life. The first year clean was actually the hardest.

After that, Jackie found a great woman to take some of the pressure off of my watchdog eyes. Gilda was also a talented musician, and I had never seen a happier couple.

Gilda was a Nashville-raised African American goddess, with a love for music, books, and Jack. The two met the night before Jack's two years sober party, at a coffee house, where the artist and music types hung out. After that, Gilda and Jack were inseparable.

The next year was all about making music and spending time with Gilda. Jack was happy and healthy, and we all got along swimmingly. Everything was great until Gavin stopped by to say that he was selling his record company to one of the bigger dogs.

Gavin admitted that he couldn't guarantee Jack the record deal he promised. Jack was just four months away from his projected goal. I understood Gavin's position, but it didn't stop me from wanting to punch him in the mouth. Of course when I actually did it, I knew there was zero chance of Jack's album getting released.

"Fuck Gavin, fuck music and fuck the wagon. This is where I get off," Jack screamed, as he stormed out of his apartment with Gilda hot on his heels.

I knew she had more leverage to talk him down. After knocking Gavin's left front tooth out, I really didn't have room to judge anyone's decisions. I wanted nothing more than to see this thing pay off, but I couldn't blame Jack for needing a drink. I need five or six myself.

I had just popped the cork on my secretly stashed champagne, when Gilda and Jack came back in. Jack made a B-line for the bottle and snatched it from my hands. Gilda and I both looked on as he threw it though the 3rd floor window, without even opening the window first.

"I have come too damn far to give up now. I have written over 60 songs waiting, and I think we can find a new record deal."

Jack became a new kind of scary at that point. He was obsessed with getting his demos perfected. He didn't have the sure thing anymore, and he had to work hard to get his foot in the door. He still refused to play bars, because of the temptation of the booze, but he started playing all-ages venues, just hoping someone would recognize his talent and hard work.

It paid off. He was recognized and offered a lot of gigs.

Jack wanted to get the hell out of Nashville. He said the scene was supersaturated. He wanted to be in Seattle. Nothing else would do. So I agreed to help him move, but Gilda refused to move with him. Her mother was really sick, and she was concerned that Jack was becoming obsessed with a record deal. Nothing else mattered to him.

Jack's mature way of dealing with her concerns was to leave her behind.

Gilda's mom passed away a few months later, but she wasn't interested in following the guy that had left her behind. Jack didn't even come back come back for the funeral. It was possible that he never got word of her mother's death, but neither of us heard from him, and on the three year anniversary of his sobriety, Jack called me to say he had a surprise. He told me to meet him at room 15 of a hotel outside of Indianapolis. He said that he was going to show me what three years of sobriety had done for him.

A million things raced through my head. I wondered if he had finally gotten his deal, and if so, with whom, and why hadn't I heard it through the grapevine. I knew he had written at least three albums worth of music. I thought maybe he had decided to record it himself and start his own little record label.

At the hotel-

I could see that the door to room number 15 was

open. Once I was inside, I could see the decorations of one hell of a party. The incredible thing was that Jack had produced his own three disc CD collection, and that included almost every song he had written during his three years sober. He had them laying all over the beds, the floor, table, nightstands and windowsills.

"Hey, buddy! Are you here?"

The disc jacket was a simple white cover with a pile of a broken instruments. I recognized most of them as Jack's personal collection. The only words printed on the case, besides the track lists, were the three words: *Three Years Sober*.

There was only one thing missing from the party—Jack. It would be just the way things go for him to have to take a shit right as I got there. From the smell of it he had been eating something rotten.

I walked over to the bathroom door. "Hello? Jackie, I think it's time to celebrate. You need to wipe your ass and get a move on it. You fuckin' did it, brother!"

I remember pushing the bathroom door open, and knocking an empty pill bottle across the floor. There in the bathtub was Jack. He had cocaine in his beard, around his open mouth, like a powdered doughnut.

The remains of a joint were still sitting in an ashtray on the edge of the tub.

I had to look away, but I didn't cry. I think a part of me knew to expect it. It was the way a rock legend would go out, if they never got a real record deal.

I sat down on the toilet next to my best friend and picked up the boom box from the floor. Inside was the first disc of *Three Years Sober*. I was just about to push play when I heard Gilda come into the hotel room.

"Jack? Jackie are you here?"

I didn't answer her or even warn her of the nightmare she was about to see. I just pushed play on the boombox and let my tears fall as the first song began. To my surprise, Gilda didn't freak out. She just came into the bathroom with me and sat down on the edge of the tub.

We cried together and listened to all three discs of *Three Years Sober*, before we finally called the police and an ambulance. There wasn't anything they could do to save Jack, but that wasn't why he had asked us there. He called us to that hotel room to hear his music one last time with him and we did.

In a weird way I still have Jack. He is alive and well on three compact discs called *Three Years Sober*, and I listen to those discs every time I visit his grave. It's my way of dealing with life without him. It may not be normal, but I wasn't really a mourning person.

10

I pulled up to Jack's grave and got out of the car but I had forgotten to grab a corkscrew. I usually put away a bottle of wine every time I came to visit my friend. I'd pour him out a little but I didn't share much since I needed it worse than he did.

Without any way to open the wine I'd bought, I just sat on the ground and smoked a cigarette.

The cemetery was on the other side of town from my apartment. I hadn't been going as much as I did when Jack's grave was fresh, but the drive home from Destiny's wedding gave me a long drive from Indy to Terre Haute, to think. I thought about a lot of things but the only person I felt like I could talk to about them was my dead friend.

Jack was horrible at making decisions. That was why he was in the ground. But he was a great listener. I would usually ramble on to him when I didn't feel like bothering living people with my bullshit.

He never had anything to say, thankfully, but I always felt a little better when I left the cemetery.

"I think I fucked up again, my friend."

Nothing.

I took another drag from my cigarette. "I finally told Destiny everything I've been feeling. I feel like a dick because I decided to wait until she was already married. I got a little too drunk, and I made a real ass of myself, but it's all out there now."

Nothing.

"It wasn't all bad, though. I got to hang out with Alice. She's still as hot as ever. She's pretty fucking cool and I might even stand a chance with her, if I can get my shit together."

Nothing.

"She kissed me."

Nothing.

"We fucked too. She's a total freak."

Nothing.

"Not really, I made that up but we did kiss."

Talking to Jack's headstone wasn't the same without the verbal lubrication of the wine. I could have kicked myself for forgetting the wine opener. I didn't condone drinking and driving, but I still did it all the time. I didn't visit Jack often enough to keep an opener in the car.

"I value these conversations, Jack"

The other part of my visits to Jack was listening to *Three Years Sober* every time, but before I could get the first CD ready, I noticed an orange, beat-up AMC Gremlin zipping through the graveyard. I didn't recognize the car, but it seemed to me like it was heading in my general direction. I couldn't think of anyone who would be looking for me but when the car came to a stop next to mine I realized that the driver wasn't looking for me, but they were there to visit Jack too.

The driver was Jack's ex-girlfriend Gilda Nash.

I was happy to see her, and the smile on her face

told me that she was happy to see me too. I was also happy to see that she had brought a bottle of wine and a corkscrew. We seemed to have the exact same idea, but she had also brought a picnic lunch, along with fruit salad, hummus and some kind of organic crackers. Gilda was the perfect person to talk to. I had known her for years. We had a past but we cared about each other, and she was there when things went down with Jack.

11

When Jack died, I spent a lot more time with Gilda. I was still in school and spending through my student loans fast. I wanted to be with Destiny but she was busy with her own life. I figured the last thing she needed was to babysit a whiny, depressed loser. Gilda was a free spirit. She was care-free and unattached.

She also shared my feeling about Jack. We would just sit around smoking weed and listen to records or revisiting Three Years Sober together. It was nice to spend time with someone, and not have to worry about crossing the dreaded romantic barriers.

She said she liked spending time with me and that she never wanted to date another musician.

Gilda's dad was Zebadiah "Nashville" Nash, an old blues guy. He was very popular in the Nashville area. He opened and played on stage with many of the greats. He had a sound that was comparable to Son House or Muddy Waters, but he never made it to their level success.

I met a ton of good folks and interesting characters

every time we were together, but the craziest of all was the guy I affectionately called Drug Dealer Dave. Dave was a super nice, super naked guy, that lived somewhere in the hills. He had a face like a catcher's mitt and dirty blonde hair, but since he sold drugs and he was hung like John Holmes, chicks dug him. I didn't understand it, but I liked the guy.

At first I was thrown off by him and his perpetual nudity, but the more we smoked weed, the less I noticed his dangling member. It wasn't that Dave didn't own clothes. He just loved the freedom of being naked. If he was ever compelled to wear clothes at home, he would wear a teal, fuzzy bathrobe, but he never saw fit to tie the damn thing closed.

Dave had been left more money than he could ever spend, and a huge house, when his parents died in a horrific boating accident. We called it the Davecave. It was the cool place for artist types to just chill. We would sit around drinking, smoking, and listening to Dave talk for hours.

He was always going on about the corruption of modern politics and religion. Afterwords, he would always invite people to crash. I may have passed out once or twice, but I never felt comfortable enough to fall asleep there on purpose.

Being around Dave and Gilda was a nice change of pace. It was the way I imagined college life. Every night was a party.

My favorite party at Dave's house was the night Gilda pulled me into the den, away from most of the other party guests. There was a group of earthy looking hipsters in the den. They were all gathered around an expensive bottle of absinthe and an acoustic guitar. They all insisted I sit, as Gilda played a few songs, including one Jack had written about her on his *Three Years Sober* album. I loved it.

When the bottle was empty and the songs were finished, Gilda and my new friends suggested we play spin the bottle. I didn't think adults still played spin the bottle. I wasn't really interested, but the dope and alcohol had made me lazy, so I stayed. I was lucky enough to be the last person to spin it, and no one else had landed on me, but my spin meant I was going to have to lock lips with someone. All I could do was close my eyes and let it go.

I held my eyes shut even after I heard the bottle stop spinning, but when I finally opened them Gilda was looking at me, with those big brown eyes. She smiled and glanced down at the bottle. As sure I was sitting there, it was pointed at her. I took a few deep breaths, working up the courage to kiss her. It didn't have to mean anything, but at the moment everything felt extra heavy. That was when I realized that my feelings for Gilda were stronger than I want to deal with.

I moved at the pace of a turtle with a broken leg, but she moved in for the steal. I couldn't even let my mind roam. I was completely focused on her plush lips. I tried to feel guilty, but it felt natural to kiss her. Time didn't just hang in the air, but it seemed like several minutes had passed before we both fell back to our seats.

The game ended shortly after our lengthy kiss, but neither one of us ended up leaving Dave's house that evening. We stayed in the room she had adopted on the second floor. Like most of my physical encounters with women, the night was hazy. I slipped in and out of earth-moving moments. At one point, it even seemed like I was just a spectator of two bodies connecting on every level, but that may have been the amazing pot Dave gave us.

Gilda was in a class all her own. Not only was she my dead best friend's girl, but she was also crazy as a hell. Gilda was the type of girl to just do anything she wanted, when she wanted to do it. She didn't really have anything to loose, but her bigger concern was enjoying life. After Jack and her mother died, Gilda grabbed life by the balls, and said "take me where I want to go!" I think she may have been afraid of death, not that she'd never let it show. She was more focused on living for the moment, and she couldn't be tied down.

It was her wild nature that led to an unforgettable evening. Gilda and I had been on a drug-induced crazy train, and neither of us had given any consideration to where we were headed. I assumed our strange relationship would run its course, while I figured out my feelings for Destiny, but Gilda had different ideas.

Gilda and I messed around a couple times after that, but I think we both understood I wasn't anything serious. It just didn't seem right since she was practically Jack's unwed widow. Being involved with her made me feel like a creep. I liked her a lot. Spending time with her was when I was the happiest. I didn't even think about Destiny, when I was with Gilda, but the creep feeling made things weird. When things got weird, I pushed her away and moved back home to live with my mom and her new family, to hide from my feelings.

Dave offered to let me stay with him but it didn't seem like a safe or realistic option. School was over and I didn't have a place to stay, and it felt like my only option was to run home to my mommy. My mother was biologically obligated to offer me a place to stay until I got on my feet.

I didn't want to be there any more than she or her husband wanted me there, but she offered anyway. It was an offer I accepted only after much hesitation.

It was an arrangement that didn't last long.

12

I had been through a lot since the last time I had seen Gilda, but it was nice to have her back in my life. It was a surprise to see her in the cemetery, but it was even more of a pleasant surprise when she said that she had just moved to town. She had changed a lot from the time we had spent together before, but she was still one of the coolest people I knew.

Gilda had chopped off her dreads and developed a cute little fro. She also seemed to be a lot more focused on her music, and less on living for the moment. It seemed like everyone was growing up but me.

After we sobered up, we headed back to Gilda's apartment. It really wasn't anything like the Jimi Hendrix hideaway I was expecting. It was simple, just a regular apartment, with books everywhere. Most of her books were by Ayn Rand, Herman Hess, Sylvia Plath, and other famous authors I had heard of but never read. She didn't have a television, she just had books, a wine rack, a record player and a great selection of records.

We talked about old times and had a couple glasses

of wine while Gilda made us something to eat. She cooked a Thai coconut soup, which she said was called Tom Kha Phak. The ingredients were coconut milk, shiitake mushrooms, kaffir leaves, carrots, and sweet potatoes. I had never had anything like it before, and it was delicious.

Gilda served the soup with fried flat bread. She made a dip for the bread that was mostly extra virgin olive oil, herbs, and crushed red pepper. She said she hated fast food, and loved cooking interesting dishes of different ethnic and cultural foods at home. Everything she fed me was incredible tasting, and her mad cooking skills only made her more interesting and more attractive to me.

All good food and good wine aside, I felt guilty for having those kind of feelings about Gilda. It still felt wrong but she had a point when she mentioned that it wasn't about Jack. She and I were still living and breathing. If Jack wanted to be with her, he would have still been alive and with her. There was really nothing wrong with Gilda and me having connections, of whatever kind we chose.

When we finished eating, we took our wine into the living room. She sat on the couch while I fingered through her record collection. I picked out several records that I wanted to her play for me, and she picked out a few that she said I needed to hear. It was nice and relaxing to just smoke weed and listened to records.

We listened to Simon and Garfunkel's *Bridge Over Troubled Water* and smoked dope. We only listened to the first side of the record once, but we must have listened to side 2 a hundred times. Restarting the second side seemed like less work than flipping the album over.

I got equally excited every time 'The Only Living Boy In New York' started. "I love this song!" I would exclaim and smile at her.

We probably talked about music and bullshit for hours. She had read a lot of books. Her enthusiasm about the subjects and the authors made me want to read more. She offered to lend me a couple books. I agreed, but I wasn't really the kind of guy to sit around reading much more than a magazine on the toilet.

Gilda was really into reading. She knew as much about books as she did about music, food, and life itself. I was willing to listen to her talk for days, but I melted hearing her sing along to the records.

I had always loved Gilda's voice. She had the sexiest, throaty voice. She sounded like an angel who had been smoking and drinking for several years. It gave her a real Janis Joplin meets Lauryn Hill sound when she sang.

I liked listening to her talk about anything and everything. We even agreed on most of the things we discussed. I didn't always know the books she was talking about, but I was able to follow the conversation. The only thing I couldn't follow was the idea of not eating meat.

"I'm a vegan," she said. "I don't eat meat or wear leather and other animal products."

"Isn't a vegan one of those tree huggin' witches?."

"No, you're thinking about pagans. A vegan is a person who doesn't eat meat or dairy."

"It sounds a lot like a vegetarian to me," I laughed. "I think you're nuts. I love a good, bloody steak!"

"It is a lot like being a vegetarian, but since I'm lactose intolerant, I avoid dairy. I decided if I could have that much self-discipline, I could go the extra mile and avoid all animal products. I'm pretty sure animals don't like to be eaten about as much as I wouldn't want to be eaten."

"You know Hitler was a vegetarian, right?"

"Oh, really! You're going to go there?"

"What? I'm just saying vegetarians can't be trusted."

"Screw you. You're wrong. I read that the first person to compare someone they don't agree with to Hitler or a Nazi has lost the argument, due to ignorance and zero point of reference," Gilda laughed. "Besides, I'm not a vegetarian. I'm vegan, and even if I wasn't lactose intolerant, I still wouldn't eat dairy products.."

"Okay, I'll take the bait. Why can't you eat dairy products?"

"I'd hate to bore you, or get into a conversation that makes you judge me, more than you already are."

"Will you just explain the dairy products thing?"

"I'm sure you'll just find it ridiculous, but I also don't eat dairy products because of the treatment of the cows during the process."

"Aw! Come on, from where I'm sitting, it can't be that bad to be hooked-up to a machine that sucks on you all day. I'd almost pay to be mistreated like that."

"Thanks again for that mental image. My point is, do you know how they get those cows to produce so much milk?"

"I'm not a dairy scientist, but I'd guess they squeeze it out of their tits."

"They're called utters, silly."

"Whatever."

"What I am trying to tell you is that these dairy cows can only produce milk if they keep producing calves," Gilda hissed. "Those cows are locked in little cells, forced to get fucked by some bulls, and then they give birth in those little cells too. Then those calves are usually sold into the veal market, all to produce milk."

"So, what's the big veal?"

"If you weren't such an asshole you might actually be funny."

"What can I say? It's a blessing and a curse."

"It doesn't scare you to know what they do to the

meat you're eating?"

"I don't really care. It takes a lot to scare me."

"What does scare you, besides commitment?"

"I never said I was afraid of commitment."

"You don't have to. It's obvious."

"I'm not afraid of commitment. I'm only afraid of snakes and dinosaurs. Fuck reptiles!"

"You do know dinosaurs are extinct, right?"

"I don't care. If I ever saw one I'd shit my pants. They're terrifying, even in movies," I said. "What about you? What scares the hell out of you?

"No, I can't say. I'm absolutely not telling you."

"Why the Hell not? I told you," I jabbed. "Where's the fairness in that?"

"Fair? What does fair have to do with anything."

"What do you want me to tell you? Fair is fucking fair. Now just tell me."

"Alright, I'll tell you, but you'll just laugh."

"Probably, but tell me anyway."

"You promise not to laugh?"

"No."

"Fine. That little glove guy from those Hamburger Helper commercials."

"Are you kidding me?" I laughed, "I can honestly say I've never heard that one before!"

"No, really, I use to have nightmares about that Hamburger Helper Glove attacking me and grinding me up into meat for dinner."

"That certainly explains why you're a vegetarian."

Gilda gave me a playful punch in the shoulder. "Aren't you clever?"

"Not really, but I want you to know, I'm trying very hard to be good. I'm not making any sexual jokes out of you not eating meat."

"Oh! Well, sexually I still eat meat. I'm just really picky about whose meat I eat, but I think every healthy woman needs some of that meat in her life."

"Following that logic, I can honestly say I don't eat the meat. I've never even tried it. My father loves it, but I'm a strict vaginatarian."

"That's good to know," Gilda laughed. "That's about as lame as me having the Hamburger Helper Glove for my worst nightmare."

"Yeah, but I have to admit, I think I was living my worst nightmare. My life was pretty shitty. Present company and experience excluded. I don't know what I'm doing, or where I'm going and I'm not getting any younger. Everyone seems to be moving on and doing stuff with their life but me."

"I had to move on. I didn't want to end up like my mom or dad."

"They produced you, so they can't be all bad."

"My mom died. She lived a pointless life," Gilda said. "She never went anywhere or did anything. She was a great mom and wife, but it was one sided. She and dad had a loveless marriage, he was always on the road with his band. He had a woman in every zip code, and now my dad is in a home and I can't even hate him. It would make me feel like a bad person."

"What happened with your dad? What kind of home is he in?"

"He's in a nursing home in Nashville. He has a horrible case of Alzheimer's. It's pretty sad really. He doesn't even know who I am half the time. He keeps hitting on me and trying to grab my ass. It's too much. I had to get out of there."

"Why here? What makes a person move to the asshole of America?"

"I don't know. It's far enough away, but still close enough that I can get back to Nashville in a few hours if I need to. You and Jack always talked about this place like it was so boring. I need a little boring in my life. I just want to chill and write some music. I thought I might find you here. I thought I'd try it out here and see if something clicks. If nothing clicks, I can pack up and keep going until I find what works for me."

"You actually wanted to find me?"

Gilda smiled. "Of course. You are one of the few people on the planet I care about. We click."

"I agree. I think you might be the single most interesting person I've ever met, and I know a lot of weird people. I can see why Jack was so into you."

"Thank you, but I've been meaning to tell you, we don't always have to talk about Jack. I want to get t know you. We both loved Jack, but we need move beyond our lives with Jack," Gilda said. "Jack didn't even know the person I am today. I didn't find myself and what made me who I am now until Jack died. I decided I wanted to live my dreams. I embraced the things I loved, and started making my own music. That's who I am. There's more to me than Jack's girlfriend that he left behind. There's more to you, too. You're more than the best friend who thinks he needs to follow him to the grave."

"I guess you're right. I've never really thought about it like that."

"You should. I'm sure you have something inside you dying to get out. You can be incredible, too."

"You'd be surprised how often I hear that. I'm not sure how or why people seem to think I have all of this potential."

"You do. It's easy to see. You're passionate about things. I know that for a fact. You just need to stop drinking it away or wasting it on people who don't deserve you. Do something with it, for you and the people who love you."

"I think it's funny that people see so much potential in me, but I don't even know what I want to do with myself. The only thing I'm really good at is getting fucked up and doing stupid shit."

"I'm sure you have more to offer than that. I know for a fact you're good at more than that and I know whatever you decide to do, I'll be supportive, and you're going to be great at it."

"I'm glad you know I have more to offer, because I'm not nearly as sure of myself as you seem to be. I wish you'd tell me what you think I'm so good at."

"I was hoping I wouldn't have to tell you. You said you were a strict vaginatarian."

When her words left her mouth, I was speechless but I let my actions speak volumes. I awkwardly moved in to kiss her. Her lips were full and soft with anticipation. She was the best kisser I had ever locked lips with, but we didn't stop there. It wasn't long before I got lost in her warm, mocha-colored skin.

In my life, I'd had sex with a few women, but being with Gilda didn't feel like fucking. It felt like making love. There was a difference, and I would have been happy to stay inside her, and with her for the rest of my days.

The next day was my birthday, and I was excited to spend it with Gilda. She had no trouble falling asleep, but I reclined in Gilda's bed, with my arm around her sleeping body, looking up at the ceiling. It was a perfect moment, and I was too excited to sleep.

I knew I needed sleep, though, and I thought about how I use to count sheep as a kid. It was something my grandma taught me, but after the vegetarian conversation with Gilda, I couldn't stop thinking about all of the brutalized and murdered animals. My mind wondered to the lamb I had eaten, how it was sliced into delectable pieces for human consumption. Before I knew it, I was visualizing mangled sheep corpses leaping over my bed, like when I had counted sheep as child, but in a more horrific scene.

It killed me to crawl out of Gilda's bed. It was so comfortable, and despite my other bedroom activities, I couldn't recall the last time I had just stayed in bed with a beautiful woman all day.

We had made plans to have lunch together for my birthday, but we didn't go to sleep until dawn, and we had slept through the lunch hours of the day. We ended up deciding to settle for dinner at one of her favorite restaurants. After my dream, I was fine with anywhere that didn't serve meat.

Gilda took me to a little vegan restaurant. It was called Halcyon Vegan Cafe. I didn't even know the place existed. I knew about the health food store attached to it, but I had never been interested in anything they had to sell me. I had probably driven past it a hundred times or more.

The building was a Chinese restaurant when I was kid, but a lot of the area had changed, and the China Buffet had been turned into a vegan eatery, owned by the same folks who owned the health food store. It didn't look like much from the outside, but inside it looked like a bohemian Shangri-La with beads, fabric and ornate little statues everywhere. It was like something out of Octopussy.

Gilda had the ELT, a sandwich of eggplant fried to taste like bacon, with lettuce and tomato. I wasn't sure I wanted anything on the menu, but I got the Facon Veggie Burger. The menu claimed that it tasted "just like a bacon cheeseburger without all the murder."

I liked that the restaurant played the self-titled Beatles album while we were there. The whole experience was enjoyable. The burger was good and the people were really nice. They were nothing at all like the pretentious vegan hippies I had expected.

When we finished our dinner, we went back to my

place and opened one of the nicer bottles of wine I hid from myself. I had nice little collection of fine wines which I rarely got into just to get drunk. I kept plenty of cheap shit around for that. I had a British Champagne, because the British, unlike most French, believe that Champagne is better with age. I didn't really like champagne. I was much more proud of the rest of my collection. It wasn't the best, but I had a good midrange California Cabernet Sauvignon, a Turnbull Syrah, a German Riesling, a good Chianti, an inexpensive 2000 Bordeaux, a midrange Bordeaux from the same vintage, and my personal favorite, a Saintsbury Pinot Noir. I don't know who I was trying to impress with my collection, but I had developed a palate for wine after my grandmother passed away.

I had blown a lot of my inheritance from my grandmother on wine. I wanted to know the difference between Save-A-Dime shit and a nice bottle. I easily spent $5,000 or more for my wine education. I never took any classes. I just talked to the people at the wine store and bought what they suggested, and tried a lot of different wines. I thought a fine standard in wines might lead to a higher standard in other things, but I just fell back into budget wines and bar stool bimbos.

Some assholes gave me shit about drinking wine instead of beer. They said dumb things like, "Wine is for women, and why don't you drink a beer like a man?"

The main reason was pretty simple. Most of the usual beers had only 9% alcohol. Most wines have 13.5% alcohol.

Unless these dudes got a nasty lite beer, they were gulping down tons of calories. I don't really care about the pounds put on by the calories.

So a beer drunk turned a person into a fat bastard. A wine drinker got drunk faster without the bloated feeling.

My other reason was because wine tasted better. There were nights where I was just looking for a good buzz and didn't care how I got it, but most of the time I wanted to drink something I could enjoy. I didn't want canned goat piss, spicy gasoline-flavored death, and I didn't want sugar saturated fruit punch. I liked dry red wines that didn't taste like Kool-Aid.

Of course, wine didn't pack the punch that hard liquor did. Rum, whiskey, and other spirits did the trick quicker than wine, but I didn't know anyone who drank tequila or vodka because they liked the flavor. Usually, they were only looking for a certain kind of drunk. That kind of drunk was harder to recover from, and it was easy to lose your shit and peak way too early. I liked my mellow wine drunk. It made me more of lover than fighter.

Maybe if more men became wine drinkers, they would be better lovers. I wouldn't claim to be that kind of lover, but I loved getting a good wine buzz, and spending some time with a lady. Wine and a sexy woman really made it worth putting the time in to pleasing a woman correctly.

I kept those few nice bottles around in case Destiny or any other respectable woman wanted to have anything to do with me. I thought I might even stand a chance with the sexy salesperson from the pretentious liquor store across town, but she was just flirting to sell me cases of pricey wines. She didn't actually have any real interest in me.

Having Gilda over to celebrate my birthday seemed like a great reason to open one of the nicer bottles. I almost went for the Pinot, but I wanted to save it for something a little more spectacular than my birthday. I opted for the Chianti instead. Gilda assured me that she wouldn't be able to taste the difference, but after only a sip, she could tell that there was a lot more to the body and flavor of what she was drinking and she liked it.

Sharing a birthday bottle with Gilda made for a great way to spend a night. We opened a couple birthday bottles, drank wine and talked. We talked until the sun came up and we both passed out on the couch.

Birthdays now didn't have the same luster that they did when I was a kid. I had never really had a crazy birthday party as a kid, but all birthdays were leading up to the milestones of 16, 18, and 21. None of them mattered after the 21st. After that, birthdays were just a reason to take the day off of work and get drunk. In some cases it was a good way to get free drinks.

My 21st birthday was the best. I didn't have anyone to go out with. All of my friends were too busy with their own shit, so I went out by myself. I ended up drinking with girl who was also celebrating her 21st birthday. Her name was Dara. She was the only other girl I almost fell in love with.

13

My dad once told me that there are two types of people in the world. 1.) The people who save their bubble wrap, in case they ever need it to send a package. 2.) The cool kids who pop the bubble wrap, making sure it's thoroughly destroyed, while they annoy the shit out of the first type.

Dara was a type 2, in my book.

We were nearly the only two people in the bar. We each sat at our own end, with several chairs between us. I had noticed her when I got there, sitting alone, in her baby blue cardigan, green skirt, and turquoise Chuck Taylors. She had her black, indigo-tipped hair pulled back with a Melissa Joan Hart style headband. She was unmistakably cute, but it was her Modern Lovers shirt that caught my attention.

The Modern Lovers were a proto-punk band influenced by The Velvet Underground. Members of the band went on to be a part of the The Cars and Talking Heads, but the Modern Lovers only had short runs in 1970 to 1974. Lead singer Jonathan Richman used the name with several other backing bands as Jonathan Richman and The Modern Lovers, but had never made it big.

Richman eventually gravitated towards more of a low-key, folk rock style. His music wasn't completely obscure. People who knew about The Modern Lovers were really into it. I loved all things Jonathan Richman, but it was odd to see someone wearing a t-shirt of the band.

She had a real Ani Difranco meets PJ Harvey thing about her. She looked like she could have been in a band, or that she shopped out of the Salvation Army donation bin. I had a thing for indie artist rocker types. Whatever it was about her made me realize that I had a type. I usually ignored any type-casting. I welcomed the attention of nearly any one who paid me attention, but I couldn't take my eyes off of the Modern Lovergirl.

I must have been looking a little too long, because she finally turned her eyes to me. "You should take a picture, it'll last longer."

"I don't think I've heard that since the 8th grade. I wasn't looking at you," I lied. "I was trying to see the jukebox."

"Bullshit. I could almost hear your internal monologue out loud."

"I might have been looking at you a little. I was admiring your Modern Lovers shirt."

"Nice. You were looking at my chest. This just keeps getting better and better. Would you like one more chance to shove your foot in your mouth?"

"Nope. I think I'll just enjoy my drink in peace."

"If you keep looking for another three minutes, you're going to have to buy me a drink."

"What are you drinkin'?"

"Anything with roofies in it."

If anything, I could say the girl was a rare type, but

I ignored her unusual comment."I'm drinking whiskey. Does that work?"

"Does it have date rape drug in it?"

"Sorry, I left those in my fraternity jacket."

"Damn. I guess it'll have to do then."

I ordered us each a glass of whiskey and put a few dollars in the jukebox. I picked a few songs to feel out her taste in music. I went with a selection that included everything from the Eels and Dum Dum Girls to the Vaselines and The Velvet Underground. The last song I picked was the only Modern Lovers song on the song list. I wanted to see if she really knew the band or if she was just wearing the shirt.

After the music started, I went back to my drink and my end of the bar. I expected her to ignore me. We hadn't gotten off to a good start, and she seemed even more socially awkward than I was. It was off putting, but I figured it was just a front. It was good for a woman at a bar alone to have a 'fuck you' front. It weeded out the assholes, like me.

She took the whiskey, asked for three cherries, dropped the cherries in, and shot the whole glass, without even a thank you. I didn't drink mine as fast. I wasn't really a whiskey drinker. I was looking to get drunk, but I wasn't looking to get sick or arrested.

I started to sip my drink, when the lady made her way to my end of the bar. She carried her empty glass with her, and I was pleased to see her singing along with Lou Reed, as The Velvet Underground's 'Femme Fatale' filled the air.

"Hey," she said, "do you know how much a polar bear weighs?"

"What?"

"Just play along. Answer the question. Do you know how much a polar bear weighs?"

"I don't know. How much does a polar bear

weigh?"

"Enough to break the ice. Can I buy your next drink?"

"Oh, my God. I hope you know how lame that is," I chuckled.

"I was just trying to be funny. I didn't want you to think I was some weird bitch."

"It's fine. I do think you're weird, but I'd already formed that opinion from your social awkwardness, and way before your attempt at an icebreaker. Does that even really work?"

"Hey! I may be socially awkward, but I've never even used that polar bear thing before. I just thought it was funny."

"It did get a chuckle out of me. I'm not sure, but I think this may be the most I've smiled in months."

"See, aren't you glad I started this conversation? If I had left it up to you, I would've been waiting the rest of my life, and you would have never heard my spectacular polar bear icebreaker."

"I'm fairly certain I could have lived the rest of my life without hearing your icebreaker."

"Anyway, thanks for the drink. I'll get the next round."

"That's not necessary," I assured her.

"I'm Dara, and I'll be your date for this evening."

I could already feel a little buzz starting. "Jeez, you are an incredibly forward little sociopath aren't you?"

"That's not very nice. We're off to a very bad start here, Mr.-"

"Harlow, my name is Harlow. I'm sorry. I'm just trying to get drunk and not get into any trouble tonight."

"That doesn't sound any fun. Are you drinking to celebrate, or to forget?"

"A little of both, I think."

"Now we're getting somewhere. I'm celebrating,

too. What are you celebrating?"

"I just turned 21. It seemed like going to the bar was the thing to do."

"Holy shit! It's your birthday?"

"Yep. 21-"

"It's my birthday too!"

She jumped up on her bar stool and got the bartender's attention away from whatever game he was watching. She told him it was my birthday and implored him to give me a free drink too. She had already had hers, but she insisted that we each have one, due to the "absolutely awesome nature of sharing a birthday." The bartender already knew it was both of our birthdays. He had looked at our IDs. He just didn't give a shit, but he agreed to give us each a double shot of cheap whiskey, if Dara got down from the bar.

We shot our doubles, and suddenly Dara and I were best friends.

"Wouldn't it be weird if we were actually twins separated at birth," she said, leaning into me.

"That would be pretty weird, but I'm pretty sure that's not the case. I only had one sibling, a brother, and he died the day I was born."

"Damn. That sucks!"

"You're telling me. My family life only gets more fucked up from that point on."

"I'm sorry, but you're depressing. I don't think I should talk to you anymore. I'm trying to get drunk and enjoy my birthday."

"You've got a point. I'll try to keep my melancholy bullshit tucked away for one night. Tonight, we drink and listen to good music."

Warren Zevon's 'My Shit's Fucked Up' finished playing just as I was about to say how much I liked the song. There was a little pause in the music, and 'Pablo Picasso' by The Modern Lovers started. I had already had enough whiskey to start singing along. I didn't sound anything like Jonathan Richman, but it didn't stop me from trying. Dara laughed at me and pointed to the jukebox.

"I'll assume you played this on purpose. You were probably trying to see if I actually knew the band, or if I was just wearing a random band shirt, huh?"

"You've completely busted me out. That's exactly what I did."

"I'm not sure we're off to a good start. Maybe we should start over."

"I guess your mom never told you not to talk to strangers, huh?"

"Hell no, my mom brought'em home from the bar every weekend. For the record, you stopped being a stranger when you told me your name."

"I thought we were starting ov-" I began, before her words actually sank into my thick skull. "I hate to be presumptuous, but you just invite me back to your house?"

"No, but I might if you play your cards right. I don't think my boyfriend will mind."

"Oh, fuck! You have a boyfriend?"

"B.O.B.," she relied sharply.

"Bob?"

"Yeah, but don't worry about him. It's nothing serious," She giggled. "He just gets me off and goes back to sleep in my night stand drawer."

"I...um...what?"

"B.O.B. - Battery Operated Boyfriend. Yes, that is exactly what I mean. I was trying to make you laugh and lighten up a bit."

"Oh! You mean your-"

Dara rolled her eyes at me. "Vibrator! Yes, I'm talking about my VIBRATOR! It's not a dirty word, Harlow."

"Wow! Yeah. That's incredibly forward of you. I mean, I'm just not that use to it. Ya know?"

"Sure, it's cool. My dad was a prude too," she said. "The sex talk he gave me went like this: I'm gonna say this once, and once only: sex is a dirty, dirty thing for very bad people."

"I guess that's one way to look at it."

We both went back to our drinks. I didn't know what to say to her, and I was certain that she thought I was a total nerd. I had not done much to make myself seem very cool. I had brought up my dead brother, family issues, and got all weird at the mention of a dildo. It wasn't like me to get nervous around an attractive woman, but something about Dara made me feel like a socially retarded school boy.

Dara killed her drink first. "Do ya wanna come back to my place, or is that too forward?"

"That sounds cool. What do you have in mind?"

"Well, I'm not trying to imply that we're going to have sex. I don't just hook up with random strangers at the bar."

"I didn't assume that's what you meant. I was just saying that we should keep celebrating our birthdays together. We could watch a movie or something."

"That sounds boring, and I don't even own a TV. I didn't say we couldn't have sex. I just didn't want to be too forward again."

"I didn't-"

"I think we've already established that Bob can take care of things. I just don't want to go home alone on my birthday."

"I don't either. I'd love to go back to your place. I'm sure we can come up with some way to celebrate."

"I think we need more drinks."

"I agree. Happy birthday, Dara!"

"Happy birthday, Harlow!"

She ordered us both another drink of whiskey, and a shot of tequila. I didn't usually drink tequila, but Dara had a way of being very persuasive.

"Do you remember when I said that it would be weird if we were really twins separated at birth?"

"Yeah. That would be weird."

"I'm thinking that would be extra weird, since the first thing I thought when I saw you come in was; Wow! He's not a hideous man. I might like to make out with him."

"Thanks! You're also not hideous. I might like to make out with you, too."

"Too bad we already made plans to get drunk instead, huh?"

"I think we have accomplished that mission. I don't usually drink whiskey and I'm feeling it."

"You didn't even drink that much. We still need to hit all the other bars in town and get our free drinks there."

"Oh, Jesus! If you insist, but you're going to have to drive. I knew I was getting shit-hammered tonight. I didn't even bring my car. I walked here."

"You probably don't even have a car. I always fall for guys that don't have cars, or jobs, or the basic understanding of how to get a woman off."

"I do have a car. I might have those other things too, but it sounds like it sucks to be you. I see why you were such a jerk, when we first met."

"Something like that. Let's get out of here!"

We stumbled to Dara's car. It was a cotton-candy pink 1978 Chevy Malibu with green interior. It was clear that neither of us were in any condition to drive. Everything was spinning for me, and my speech was all kinds of slurred. It was bad, and Dara's condition was even worse. She was walking like some kind of overly dramatic secret agent, and talking with a horrible British accent. I think she might have even been humming the James Bond theme at some point.

It was clear that we didn't need to go to any more bars. We agreed that the best course of action was to stay sitting in her Barbie-mobile, until one of us sobered up enough to drive. It was going to be a while, and eventually Dara started talking to me like we were on a stake-out. Soon, we were both pretty into it. We made up bad guy names and criminal histories about the people walking by, until she leaned across the front seat and planted a kiss on my lips.

After the kiss we decided that we were sober enough to drive. We probably weren't, but we were both eager to get back to her house. It didn't seem like it took long to get there, and it wasn't at all what I was expecting.

"So, this is my humble abode. It's not much. Who am I kidding? It's a shit-hole. Don't mind the mess. I pretty much just stay in my bedroom when I have to be home. It's this way."

I looked around until she grabbed my index and middle fingers with her hand to guide me toward her bedroom.

Her unmade bed was something else. The blush-colored comforter and fuchsia blankets covering black and white striped sheets made it look like Barbie had thrown up all over a zebra. It was covered in stuffed animals and about a million pretty pink pillows. I had never seen so much pink.

"So, here it is. This is where the magic happens, or whatever they say on that stupid show. AND now I sound like a total slut. I didn't mean any magic really happens here. I was just try to be funny again."

I laughed at her attempt to be funny, but my eyes were drawn to the very detailed, pink dildo on the nightstand.

"I guess that's your...uh...um-"

"Vibrator. Jesus," she laughed. "Just say it."

Dara turned the vibrator on and offered a hand shake with it in her hand. "Harlow, this is Bob. Bob, this is Harlow."

I started to shake with the vibrator but stopped myself and looked around. I looked at anything but Dara and her vibrating little friend. It was just too damn weird.

"No thanks. I just don't want to touch it."

"That's cool, but you are going to have to lighten up if we are going to hang out. I like you, Harlow, but if this is going to go anywhere, you need to relax."

"I'm relaxed," I scoffed. "I just don't wanna touch your dildo. Wait?! What do you mean 'if this is going to go anywhere?"

"I was just saying I like you. You're nice. I might like havin' you around."

"That could be nice."

"Do you smoke?"

"Cigarettes?"

"I don't mean cigarettes. I mean, do you hang with Willie Nelson, ya know?"

"Oh, do I smoke pot? Yeah. I guess. Sometimes. Why?"

"I've got some really good stuff, from a guy I know. It's from Mexico or some shit like that. You wanna hit it...the pot...I mean do ya wanna hit a bowl, not...never mind."

"Sure. Yeah, I get what you mean. I didn't assume you meant "hit it" like that."

"Maybe I didn't. I'm going to pack a bowl, unless you'd rather me roll you a joint."

"I'm cool either way, but I have to admit you're incredibly forward. I don't know many girls like you."

"That's a good thing or you wouldn't be here now.

I'm sorry if I'm a little too forward for you. I just know what I want and I go for it. If I fuck up along the way, so fucking what? Anyway, I'm glad you're here. "

"Me, too."

Dara brought me a bowl and held it up between our faces so we stand nearly nose to nose. She smiled a sexy, sinister grin, and bit her bottom lip.

"SO, you wanna hit it?"

Dara and I both go in for a kiss and our mouths exploded together. We made out, while and wrestled with each other's clothes until we were both naked on her Barbie Dream Bed. There wasn't much foreplay. We got right into the kind of sex the neighbors had to hear.

After she rocked my world, we just stayed in bed, covered with only the fuchsia sheet, post sex, handing the bowl back and forth.

"I'm sorry I was weird about the whole vibrator thing," I said.

"It's cool. You were just nervous and needed a little 'fuck it all' in your system. I mean, a girl likes to get off. I don't see why I gotta hide that shit. I masturbate. It's a fact. People do it. I'll bet even you wax the tadpole from time to time."

"Are you kidding me? Religiously. I would be on a clock tower with a semi automatic rifle, laying waste to society if I didn't glaze a knuckle now and then. It keeps me sane. I'm not really a porn guy, though I have a pretty good imagination. It's getting out of my own head that's the problem."

"That doesn't sound like the usual everyday bullshit. That sounds like it could be interesting. I might be interested in getting into that head of yours."

"I doubt that. It's a pretty bleak place."

"It sounds like some parts could be pretty fun," Dara smiled. "My first manipulation device of choice was my Squiggle Wiggle Writer.

"That sounds familiar but I don't think I had one. I don't remember having anything with a name like that. It must have been a girl thing."

"Oh, it was! Don't you remember, it was a fat ink pen that moved and vibrated to make your handwriting all funny looking?"

"Holy shit! I remember those things! Every girl in my school had those things."

"I'm sure they did. I'm sure they used it like a vibrator too."

"That's kinda fucked up. I'll never be able to look at pens the same way ever again."

"Fucked up? I'm sorry it doesn't have the majesty and wonder of a JC PENNY catalog bra section and a bottle of Jerkins."

"Hey! Easy, I loved some of those women. I guess every guy did that. I always thought it was my secret, but didn't you worry about getting ink in your-"

"I didn't thrust the pen up in there, weirdo. I just held it against my clit, like a vibrator. My fingers did the only penetrating. You need to watch less porn. That's not how women masturbate. BUT, anyway, that was when I came up with the whole "battery-operated boyfriend," or "B.O.B." thing. I'm sure my parents thought I was writing a fucking novel."

"A 'fucking novel', huh?"

"Oh, he's got jokes. I'm glad you're coming out of your shell a little. You're funny."

We looked at each other and laughed. It felt good to laugh. There wasn't any pressure. I probably enjoyed it more than she did. I was thinking about her masturbating with a vibrating pen. It aroused me, but I didn't mention it or do anything about it. I just enjoyed the moment.

She looked at me with a nervously sincere smile, "Happy birthday."

"Happy birthday, to you, too," I replied.

We finished the bowl. It made us lazy, but that led to us spending the rest of the night in bed together. We got frisky a few more times. It was nice.

We were pretty much inseparable for a long time from that point on.

14

I had been crashing at Gilda's house on a regular basis. I even called into work to enjoy my birthday and a couple extra days with her. It took most of my vacation days, but it was worth it. Things were actually beginning to feel like a relationship. I wasn't sure if it was an official thing, though. We never had the conversation.

There wasn't any reason to talk about it if things didn't feel weird. I left it alone and things went well.

Everything was great until I had to go back to work.

I had been leaving my car at my apartment while I stayed with Gilda. She had a car, and there wasn't any reason for me to drive mine around all the time. Leaving it at home saved gas, and I didn't think I had anything to worry about, until she dropped me off at my apartment.

Someone had caused a serious amount of damage to the body, flattened all four tires, smashed out both of my headlights and thrown an open can of paint through my windshield.

Green paint dumped out of the can when it smashed my windshield. There was paint all over the hood and interior of my Chrysler. It was a cunning attack. Despite the rest of the chaos, the fucker responsible for the damage had strategically wrecked things with one can of paint. The rest of the mess was just insult to injury.

It was hard to tell how long it had been fucked up since I hadn't been home in nearly a week and I didn't know who to blame. The list of people I had pissed off was pretty long, but I wasn't sure if I had pushed anyone to the point of destroying my car. It wasn't unlikely, though.

The biggest bitch of it all was that I didn't have insurance. It just seemed like a waste of money to me. I never saw a reason to have it. I always assumed that if anything happened to my car, I could deal with it. I was a careful driver and didn't fuck up other people's shit, even when I was drunk.

"It might have just been a group of random kids just raising hell," Gilda assured me.

"I doubt that."

"What makes you think someone would do this to you intentionally? Have you made anyone mad lately?"

"I can think of a few people that don't like me very well."

"Do they really hate you enough to do something like this?"

I glared at the thing that was once my car. "I'm not sure."

"I think you're just being paranoid."

"I hope, but I doubt it, from the looks of things."

Gilda looked over the damage with me, but she didn't stay. She didn't need to. She offered me a ride to work. I refused, because I didn't work far from home and I drove a company van while I was on the clock. For the most part I wanted her to leave, because I was already thinking about calling in again, to find the sonofabitch who trashed my car.

I wasn't sure what I was going to do when I found him, but it wasn't going to be something Gilda needed to be a part of. She thought I was being paranoid, anyway. She tried to tell me that it was just teenagers being little assholes, but the paint can assault, and the timing seemed too intentional to be happenstance to me.

It wasn't hard for me to image Elmer doing something to my car. He said he wanted me out of his life, but I had pissed him off pretty bad. He wasn't the only person I had crossed in the last few years. I had a habit of pissing people off, particularly when I was drunk.

Being drunk had ended on a few positive notes, but more often it had gotten me into trouble. Looking at my car made me want to dive into a bottle of Beam. Whiskey wasn't my friend, but I didn't give a shit. I needed something stronger than wine.

15

Whiskey and I had a bitter past that all started with an email invitation to a party. It was a chain email from someone I went to high school with. I didn't pay much attention to it, but I wrote down the date before I deleted it.

I hated parties and most of the people I went to school with, but things had gone south with Dara, I was going to be home Spring break, and I wanted to see the band that was playing at the party.

Lassie and The Melancholies were a local band with no aspirations of ever making it out of the Midwest. I had seen them play in Jack's garage, and again at a 4th of July Battle of the Bands. They had influences ranging from The Violent Femmes and Patti Smith to Sonic Youth and The Kills. They had a real raw sound, and nostalgic lyrics I could relate to. They wrote about crazy parties and first loves.

I liked their music, but I was really smitten with the lead singer. Lassie's real name was Mary Jane Gomez. She had a natural olive skin tone and copper-colored hair that hung in long curls and wavy sprigs that would not be contained. Her crazy hair and the noticeable nose-ring in her left nostril gave her the indie rocker thing I liked in a woman. I didn't usually dig on facial piercings, but I dug M.J. I particularly dug her singing and dancing in her undergarments.

Nobody told me that it was an underwear party. I wore my Johnny Cash-style button-down western shirt and dark jeans. I was about the only one not stripped down to my skivvies. I thought about dressing down, but I couldn't stop looking at Mary Jane

She looked fantastic in her black bikini-cut cotton panties and lavender bra. I watched the couture of each ass cheek and the way the cotton compressed her beautiful backside. I tried not to stare, but the impression of her kitty against her undies was a thing of beauty.

I didn't want to miss a wardrobe malfunction or the slightest nipple slip.

After the band was finished playing, I worked up my courage to talk to Mary Jane. I felt like a perv, gawking at her while she was singing, but I wasn't just interested in her body. I was into everything about her. I couldn't imagine what she would ever see in me, though, and I was afraid that I'd start undressing her with my eyes, if we were ever close enough to have a conversation.

I turned to liquid courage, in the form of whiskey. It took a lot of courage to even smile when she looked my way. It took a shit-load of stupidity to keep drinking Jim Beam when she came over to talk.

We started off with small talk about high school and mutual friends, but she didn't roam off after the casual conversation was over. She stayed and talked about music, and what she wanted to do after college. I talked about music and how weird it was trying to have a normal conversation, while everyone was walking around in their underclothes.

"Why aren't you sporting the underwear-only look?"

"I'm not sure. Nobody told me it was that kind of party."

"You know now. When in Rome, take your clothes off. I'm about to get in the hot tub. You can't join me, dressed like a cowboy."

"I was going for a Man In Black, outlaw kind of thing."

She shot me a cocky grin. "Oh, I get it."

"It's not working, is it?"

"Not at all. You should probably lose the clothes."

"I've always wanted a woman to tell me that."

"Just any woman?"

"I think any guy wants any woman to tell him that, but I'm celebrating the fact that it's you telling me to take off my clothes."

"Well, celebrate by taking your pants off. I'm ready to get in that hot tub!"

"Do you dare me?"

"I double dog dare you!"

"Oh hell, this is getting serious. I think I have to do it."

"I can top that. I Snoop Doggy Dogg dare you!"

"Well, I have to do it now. That's some gangsta shit! Here I go!"

I ditched the clothes and joined Mary Jane in the hot tub. I was terrified about getting a boner and not being able to hide it within a pair of wet boxers. I prayed that if I pitched a tent in my shorts, M.J. would take it as a compliment, but it never happened.

We played a game about obscure band references. The goal of the game was to stump the other person with trivial music questions. If the other person didn't know the answer, they had to take a shot. She knew a lot more about indie music than I did, but we both ended up drunk.

The game ended happily when I got the drunken idea to be flirty. "What underwear party playing band has one of the sexiest lead singers I've ever seen in my life?"

"I don't know. I guess I'll take my shot."

"I tried to make it obvious. You really don't know?" She took her last shot. "I'd rather not say."

"I mean you. You're beautiful and talented."

"I'm sure you only think she's sexy because she's sitting in a hot tub in her panties and there is Jim Beam involved."

"Not at all. You're-"

Before I could finish my sentence, Mary Jane pulled me out of the hot tub and into the house. We made our way through the kitchen and up the stairs, but every door we opened had some body getting sick, making out, or doing the dirty. We eventually ended up in M.J.'s car, a couple blocks away, in a dark parking lot.

The windows fogged up fast. I was a little nervous about doing anything in the car. I wasn't an exhibitionist. I didn't need anyone seeing my naked white ass bouncing up and down, but she crawled into the backseat without hesitation. I knew nobody was going to see us, and when she threw her bra into my lap, I jumped into the back and into one of my favorite moments of my life. I will always remember slipping my fingers under those black cotton panties and into the waiting wetness of the warmest, softest snatch in the world.

The scene in the backseat was playing out like the scene from a Meatloaf song, but just as I was about to slide into home, someone tapped on the window.

I could tell by the flashlight that it was a cop. I couldn't understand what he said, but when I cracked the window, he told us to get dressed and take our sex life somewhere else. He didn't seem concerned with the fact that we both smelled like a distillery. He just wanted us on our way. We headed to Mary Jane's apartment.

When we got to her place, she was fumbling with her keys, while I was fumbling with her bra. We were so into making out that we fell on the floor once the door was open. We didn't even shut the door. We tried to finish getting naked and have sex right there on the floor, but I couldn't get it back up.

We stumbled on into her bedroom, and she tried everything she could to get me hard. Nothing worked. I made things worse by thinking about it. It was frustrating, but the limp little fact was that I had officially been blown down with whiskey dick.

The only way to make up for my short comings was to go down on her. Mary Jane wasn't very happy about the substitution, but she seemed to perk up when my tongue found the right spot. I was wasted, but I was still pretty sure I knew what I was doing down there.

In only a few seconds she was writhing and moaning like a hellcat. I was starting to feel confident when a wave of nausea washed over me. It was nothing against her lovely lady parts. The spinning room made me sick, and the whiskey was fighting its way back out.

I didn't even get to finish the job before I was running for the bathroom and puking in her ugly green toliet. I puked until my head fell as limp as my dick.

I rested my face on the toilet seat, until I noticed a hair in my mouth. I thought I was going to be sick again when I noticed it was a pubic hair in my mouth. It was extra gross, because I knew for a fact that MJ wasn't sporting any hair on her bathroom parts, and I hadn't used the latrine yet.

It made me curious about whose short and curly was stuck to my lip.

The rest of the night was a waste. She was a good

sport about everything. She teased me about having whiskey dick and getting sick, but she let me stay. I thought it was especially nice of her, even if she regretted it the next morning.

Mary Jane was still passed out, naked and disheveled like a rockstar, when I woke up. I checked to make sure she was alive, but I could feel a demon churning in my belly when I started moving around. I knew I was brewing either a vile fart, or something worse.

I wasn't willing to take any chances.

I crawled out of bed, carefully so as not to wake her up. I was going to try to sneak out and try to make it to my own bathroom. It was a great idea that I didn't get to execute. I was forced to answer the call of nature, or shit myself trying to escape. All I could do was clench my cheeks and sneak into her bathroom. I was doing well until I shut the bathroom door. As soon as the door clicked shut, I heard her saying something. I ignored her to release the shit silently, but when she knocked on the door she was greeted with the horrible sound of an excrement-plosion.

There is nothing on Earth that can rival the burning sensation and rancid smell of the whiskey shits. It was like a super-shit from another planet. Whiskey shits were more powerful than a pig farm, and able to out-stink cat crap in a single dump.

16

The morning after I found my car trashed-

I woke up to someone beating on my front door. It sounded like whoever was knocking was pounding on my skull. I felt like fucked hard death. My head was still swimming in whiskey and I didn't care who was at the door, but I knew if I didn't answer it, they might never stop knocking.

When I opened the door there was my dad, who was supposed to be in California. He stood there like a jackass with his arms out, expecting a hug. He was wearing khaki shorts, with a fanny pack, sandals, and his 'You're Just Jealous Because I Speak Klingon' t-shirt. He looked like the world's biggest nerd.

The apple fell very far from the tree.

I hadn't seen my dad much since he and my mom split up. He had been living in San Francisco with his boyfriend, like some homosexual stereotype. I only saw him a few times a year. He came home for Thanksgiving, Christmas, and in August when he graced the Midwest for his geek gathering in Indianapolis.

"Well, hello stranger. Are you going to invite me in?" My father squealed.

"Are you are wearing a fucking fanny pack?"

"Oh, heck yeah, but it's called a Belt Pack, now. It's cool," my father proclaimed. "It's like Batman's Utility Belt. It holds my wallet and keys, and I can even keep my dice in it."

"Oh my God! No. Fanny packs were and never will be 'cool'."

"Whatever. I think it's cool, besides, Larry got it for me."

"Larry got you a fanny pack. That is so cute." I scoffed, as I moved out of the doorway for him to come in. We went into my living room.

We sat there for at least seven or eight minutes before either of us said anything.

"So, can we get to the part when you tell me why you're here?"

"Can't a guy just want to visit his only son?" He laughed, "I just wanted to visit. I thought it might be nice to sit and talk in person. I had the money and time to come out. So, here I am."

I thought about making a joke about him "coming out." I didn't, I just let the moment pass. I also let the next moment pass while we sat on in a solid minute of silence. He didn't talk. He just looked around the apartment, and I couldn't think of anything to say. I wasn't in the mood for company. I wanted to know why my dad really flew half way across the country unannounced, but more than anything, I really just wanted to be left alone.

Dad finally broke the silence. "Do you ever see your mom?"

"Nope. I doubt she really wants to see me, after how things went the last time."

"You're probably right about that. What were you

thinking?"

I ignored his question, and turned the stupid questioning on him. "So, are you still playing with dolls?"

"They're called action figures, Harlow," he snapped.

"Yeah, right, action figures. I'm sure that's what Ken tells Barbie too."

"I don't play with them. I collect them, but I get it. I can tell when I'm not wanted," he said, standing up to leave.

"Sit down," I said. "You flew all the way here, I'm sure you have a reason."

"I just find it hard to believe that my son, the guy who wanted to be a writer, forgot how to write a letter, or pick up the damn phone."

"Geez, I'm sorry. Damn. Don't get your fanny pack in a bunch. What's going on?

"I don't really know. I don't know how to say this. I guess I'll just come right out and tell you; Larry and I broke up."

"Damn, dad. I'm really sorry. I didn't know."

"Ah, well. It's all water under the bridge, or whatever the cliché is."

"When did you guys split up? What happened?"

"I guess it's been a week ago, now," he said. "It was the most screwed-up thing, too. Of all the guys he could have left me for, he left me for a fucking woman. Can you believe that?"

"Wow, what a twisted concept. A man sleeping with a woman? That's like something out of science fiction."

"Har, Har, my son, the comedian. Have you ever thought that you're in the wrong line of work?"

"Every day, but all joking aside, I thought you guys were happy, I mean, isn't that the true meaning of the word gay?"

"Sweetheart, we haven't been happy for about a year. I was going to leave him anyway, but I'm pissed he beat me to it. I had been seeing a guy name Tracey for about four months, until he went back to his wife. I swear, I'd be a happy guy if it weren't for women."

"I'm sorry if I find that funny, too. I always thought Tracey was a girl's name."

"It's actually funny that you mention that, because the woman Larry was cheating on me with was named Tracy, without the E."

"Holy shit, what are the chances you'd both be messing around with people named Tracy? This just keeps getting more and more creepy. At least you gays didn't have a kid, like the last time your love life went South."

"Well, that's where the plot thickens, and why I've been trying to call you. The female Tracy was to be the surrogate mother of our child together, but instead of getting her pregnant the scientific way, Larry decided to go at it the old fashioned way. The rest, as they say, is academic."

I couldn't really think of a sarcastic response and that may have been for the best, because my dad was oozing unhappiness. I didn't understand if he was more upset about losing Larry, about Tracy, or Tracey and a possible second child. I didn't really understand any of it. I wanted to say something comforting, but I was drawing a blank.

Dad took a deep breath and stood up. "Grandpa Harlow isn't doing very good. I was going to the nursing home to see him, while I'm here. Wanna come with me?"

I didn't want to go at all, but I lied. "I'd be happy to go. It might be nice to spend time with ya, and I haven't seen grandpa since he went into the home."

"Good. I'm glad you wanna go. It might be your last chance you have to see him."

I wasn't sure why I agreed to go, and I really wasn't sure why I agreed to ride with my dad. He subjected me to shitty music for the entire drive. I would have asked him to turn it off, but it was his car. I would have been safer driving myself. He was more interested in singing along to the Rent soundtrack than he was interested in watching the road.

My dad was so much like every gay character on television that I had a hard time believing that he actually sucked cock. He fell into every stereotype and cliché, that I was sure it had to be an act. I thought he just wanted an excuse to leave my mom, until I had caught him and Larry mid-rim-jamming session.

That was all it took to convince me that he was the real squeal deal. No man takes it in the pooper, if he's just pretending to be gay. He was still the most cookie-cutter gay man I had ever seen. It only made sense that he had learned everything about being gay from TV.

I was sure that he had learned to drive the same way. He was such a horrible driver that I was actually happy to get to the nursing home. I was surprised that we'd finally made it without dying in some sort of horrific accident.

Dad went in first, while I tried to smoke a much needed cigarette. I only took a few drags before I stamped it out. I was nearly car sick and the smoke from the cigarette made me gag until I about puked. It wasn't worth it, and I realized I needed to follow my dad, to know where I was going.

He was already talking to hefty looking nurse when I walked in. I watched each of her ass cheeks rise and fall with each step she took. It didn't do anything for me, but it made me think about how the nurses I see never look like the sweet little sexy things in movies.

Hollywood was so full of shit. They had lied to me for years, and fed me fantasies that would never come true. The closest I'd ever come was watching my copy of Naughty XXX Nurses. Those nurses had fantastic asses, but I doubt they knew a damn thing about real nursing.

I was balls deep into thinking about nurses, when I heard my dad yell. "Nurse, help me get him up. Harlow, shut the door."

As I got to the doorway. I could see my grandpa's pale, old naked body on the floor. My dad and a nurse rushed over to help Grandpa Harlow back into his wheel chair, and get him covered. I fumbled to shut the door, but I stayed as close to it as possible. It was a strange situation and I wanted to be close to an exit if things got even worse.

The room smelled like day-old piss and mentholated muscle rub. It wasn't the smell I usually associated with my grandpa, from my time living with him and grandma. Their house was filled with the smell of vanilla candles, wood burning in the fireplace, or whatever Grandma Kingston was baking. It was usually made-from-scratch oatmeal raisin cookies or apple pie. Their house had the smell of love and tranquility.

Grandpa had a wild look in his eyes. He seemed to be in pain, but he was still full of piss and vinegar. "What? What in the hell are ya doin' here?"

He looked around without focusing on anything. He looked at my dad, but it was clear that he wasn't even sure who he was looking at. Grandpa Harlow struggled and resisted their help, until he recognized the nurse. They eventually got him into his chair with a blanket.

The nurse trotted out of the room to get his medicine. She shot me a nervous look, as she walked out of the room. I just hugged my jacket uncomfortably.

"I came to surprise you, dad, but you got me

instead," my dad laughed nervously. "Why are you naked on the floor, with your ass up in the air? How long have you been down there?"

Grandpa started shouting."What do ya think I'm doin' down there? Those damn gooks took all my money and my clothes."

"Seriously? I don't think anybody stole your money or your clothes."

"Are you calling me a damn liar? That's no way to talk to your superior officer. I know what happened. The gooks are mad about the war, and they robbed me."

"Dad, we don't call them names like that," my dad tried to explain. "Those are racial slurs. It's socially unacceptable,"

"Ah, horse shit! Don't tell me what I can and can't do. I'm-" My grandpa stopped talking all of a sudden and looked directly at me with disgusted confusion. "Who the fuck is that guy? Why's he trying to look at my testicles!"

"That's your grandson, Harlow. Don't you remember your grandson?"

My grandpa had to think for a minute or two. I wasn't sure if he was faking or if he actually remembered me, but he eventually perked up and said that he remembered me.

"Of course I remember my own grandson. I ain't no retarded. Let me look at ya boy. I think you've grown. That's all."

I walked over toward Grandpa Harlow. I was a little afraid. I didn't know what he planned to do to me and I knew he was naked under the blanket on his lap. He didn't do anything too strange. He just grabbed my arm pretty hard and spun me to get a good look at me.

"I'd bet he had a bigger dick than this kid," Grandpa laughed. "How about it, Harry? Are you a lady's man? Do you a have a girlfriend or two, or are you one of them queers?"

I wanted to tell him my name wasn't Harry. I had the same damn name as him. I was named after him. I would have thought he could have gotten my name right, but his brain had gone to shit.

Before I could correct him or say anything, my grandfather got a very serious look on his face. He squinted one eye, and produced a squishy noise that resembled a fart. When he was finished, the smell of a freshly shat wheelchair filled the air. I took it as my cue to leave the room and not go back.

Seeing my grandpa in such a state shook me up. I didn't have a lot of memories of my Grandpa, but he was always my favorite because I shared his name. He was also the original spitfire of our family. He was into heavy drinking, chain smoking, and fast women before it was cool. He had a hard life but he had brought it on himself and everyone around him. He was the guy who was more interested in drinking and fucking around than he was interested in having a family. He wasn't much of a father to my dad. He left his wife and kid and didn't get involved with either of them again until they had learned to live without him.

I didn't know that side of him. He had learned to fake the perfect life by the time I was born. He had sucked at being a dad, but he was an all right grandfather, before he lost his mind.

17

My favorite memory of spending time with Grandpa Harlow was the day he took me to the newsstand to get some comics. It was the same day I stepped into a bar for the first time. I was thirteen.

I didn't like very many superheroes that well. I was always a much bigger fan of anti-heroes or the villains. Before long, they didn't do it for me either. I mostly read a lot of Tales From The Crypt and MAD Magazine. That was when I stopped buying comic books.

I'm pretty sure Grandpa Harlow put me on that path. This was during the time when comics had to have a wraparound chrome or hologram cover, so to pick up a major issue would cost around five bucks. He planted the seed in my head that eventually turned me off of comics.

Grandpa Harlow looked at the cover of the comic, then down at me. "You know this one will cost your whole allowance, right?"

"Yeah, I know, but this is the issue where Jean Grey dies," I said, as naive as the day was long.

My grandpa just rolled his eyes. "Are you sure you don't want a Playboy, instead?"

"No way. This will be worth a lot of money someday!"

There's not a lot of dignity in jerking off, but nothing is more pathetic than jerking off to a scantily clad comic book vixen, instead of a picture of a real woman. I loved those busty women. I wish I would have gotten the Playboy.

I later sold that very comic book in a box of comics I didn't want anymore for $50, and Jean went on to die 13 more times. For once, I wish they would just kill a comic book character and leave them dead.

Looking back, there is still one thing which bothers me about a certain caped crime fighter:

If Bruce Wayne wanted to help people and fight crime, I don't know why he didn't just join the police force. He could have also donated a considerable portion of his vast millions to fighting crime. Instead, he put on spandex and swung around the rooftops with underage boys. He let the same underage boys live in his house. I always thought Bruce was gay. There wasn't anything wrong with it if he was. It would explain why he really couldn't make a relationship work with any woman.

The Bat needed to fly solo, if he was patrolling for dudes. It can't be that easy to find a hot guy who's into spandex-clad superheroes. I would imagine his plight would be even more difficult if he had to compete with a younger, hipster sidekick, sporting a bigger codpiece.

It was hard to believe that I had ever spent my money on comics, when for a few dollars more I could have bought a Playboy or, God forbid, a novel. I couldn't even think about ever buying another comic. I was a lot like my grandfather. I didn't understand the allure.

When we left the newsstand, Grandpa Harlow had

to stop for a beer. I knew I wasn't old enough to go in. My mom had told me to never go into such an awful place, but my grandpa assured me that she was crazy.

He said that he wouldn't take me anywhere that was a bad place. "Would I ever do anything to hurt you?"

"I don't think so."

"Hell, no, I wouldn't. I'm your grandpa. I have to look out for ya."

I didn't say anything. I let his words sink into my brain. I didn't fully believe him, but I wanted to trust him.

"Besides, if I let anything happen to you, I'd go to jail," he said. "Do you think I want to go to jail?'

"No."

"Then it's settled then. Quit being a little pussy. Let's go."

We got out of his Buick and started towards the door. We only made it a few steps before grandpa looked at me as serious as I had ever seen him look. He looked like he was going to cry. I could tell that he had something important to tell me before we went in.

He grabbed me by the shoulders. "I need to tell you something, but you can't tell anyone. Only my friends in here know the truth."

"Okay. You can tell me."

"I need you to promise you won't tell a soul."

"I won't tell anyone. I promise."

"I think it's only fair that I let you know the truth. You need to know that I'm really Jesus Christ."

"No, you're not. That doesn't even make sense. You can't be."

"Fine, don't believe me? Just wait until we walk in this bar. You'll see."

I didn't know what to think, but I had doubts that my grandpa knew what he was talking about. I thought he was nuts. I suddenly doubted that it was alright for me to go into the bar and I was positive that he was not Jesus.

He started to open the door and he motioned for me to go in first. I was instantly apprehensive. I had no idea what I was walking into.

"Jesus Christ, are you here again!" the bartender shouted.

My grandfather slapped me on the shoulder and started laughing. "See, I told ya! Did you hear what he called me when we walked in? He says it every time."

The bartender didn't say a word about a kid being in the bar. He and grandpa had a good laugh at my expense. They called me a little green boy and told me to belly up to the bar. It was my first time on a bar stool, and I felt like the coolest kid in the land.

The bar was a place called Pat's Place. It was a dirty hole-in-the-wall. It smelled like greasy food, cigarettes and stale beer. I didn't know what those smells were then, but I didn't like it.

Grandpa Harlow had a beer and a burger. He let me order anything I wanted. I had the fish sandwich, slaw, and a Sprite. I wanted to order a beer like my grandpa but I knew I wasn't old enough. I didn't think they'd let me have one, but my grandpa let me try his. It was the first time I tried any alcohol and I hated it.

I grew to love the taste of alcohol, as an adult, but I usually liked the way it made me feel. I had also grown to know the smells of bars very well. They smelled like home.

18

When I got back from the nursing home I was feeling pretty miserable. I hated seeing my grandpa in the state he was in, my car was still trashed, and my hangover was hanging on. It had me thinking about some pretty dark things. I thought that I was going to end up just like my grandfather, or worse. No matter how happy I was with Gilda, I thought maybe Jack was right. Maybe the best way to go out was in a hotel bathtub, from a drug overdose, like a rock star.

I really thought I just wanted to be left alone, but I changed my mind when Gilda dropped by with a cheap bottle of wine and a blunt. It was nice to see her after everything that had transpired. We made a peaceful evening of drinking, smoking, and listening to records.

She told me all about her obsession with The Animals. I had heard the songs that got radio play. Almost everyone had heard 'Don't Let Me Be Misunderstood', 'It's My Life', 'We Gotta Get Out Of This Place' and 'House Of The Rising Sun', but I hadn't paid much attention to their hard rock, or their psychedelic hits. Gilda really liked all of their music, but she was partial to those songs. She was particularly fond of 'Sky Pilot' and 'San Franciscan Night.'

She had a lady-boner for Eric Burdon. "He is everything people love about Mick Jagger and Jim Morrison, wrapped in one sexy British package. I think he's highly underrated. His voice was the best."

"If they were a part of the whole British invasion thing, would you put them over The Beatles?"

"You can't compare any band to The Beatles. They did their own thing. They were The Beatles. They did great things, changed with the times, and had successful solo careers. They were as great independently as they were together. Burdon had some success with War, but he's not the pop cultural icon that the Beatles or John Lennon was. That's not a fair question."

"People compare The Beatles and the Rolling Stones all the time. Why isn't it fair to compare The Animals and The Beatles?"

"The Animals never got all the credit they deserve. People mistake The Animals' music for The Stones and The Doors all the time."

"In your humble opinion, can you compare them?"

"The Animals were vastly more superior to The Doors. I love The Doors, but I listen to them when I'm high or drinking wine. It would be better to compare The Animals to The Stones, and it's no contest, because they are equally as good musically, but Eric Burdon is far better looking than Mick Jagger or Richards put together. He's sexy, and their music is incredible. The Animals, my favorite band."

"I think you're obsessed with this Eric guy. Maybe you should go find him."

"I've seen him before. He's getting older now. He still looks great for an older man. I think he's going into his late sixties or seventies now, and I'm not into men that much older than me."

"Lucky for me, huh?"

"Something like that. I really just wanted to show someone The Animals, I mean really show someone. I figured you could understand where I was coming from."

"I don't find them as sexy as you do, but I can respect where you're coming from, and I can hear the music. I can't call them my favorite band, but I'm going to be listening to them a little more regularly. Thank you!"

"Sometimes we need to go backwards to discover great music, instead of turning on the radio and subjecting ourselves to the shit slush pile. I can appreciate what Lady Gaga, Greyson, and Nicki Minaj are trying to do, but I can't enjoy it. I want that old time rock 'n' roll."

I couldn't have agreed more.

We drank wine and listened to records, but Gilda refused to light the blunt until I had heard every song at least twice. Seeing Gilda so excited and passionate about something was a real turn on. She really knew her shit, and even when she stated her opinion, it sounded like facts.

When I had heard The Animals and a few select Eric Burdon tracks, with commentary, we switched gears to relax. She knew who my all time favorite was and when the record started playing, she lit the blunt. We listened to Bob Dylan's *Blood on the Tracks* and smoked until we melted into each other and fell asleep on the couch.

I had only been asleep a few minutes when the harsh sound of my phone jolted me from my passed-out state. The ringing next to my ear sounded like hell's bells echoing a painful song through my head. I had obviously drunk too much the night before, and the ringing was

God's way of reminding me I was a fuck-up and a drunk.

I ignored the first couple of calls, but by the third time it started ringing, I had heard enough and finally picked up the receiver. I wish I wouldn't have answered it, because it was my step-father on the other end of the phone.

My step-father cleared his throat before he spoke. He sounded very upset. I was used to that tone in his voice. "Harlow?"

"Yeah. What's up?"

"Your mom's gone."

"What?"

"Your mom is gone."

"Okay? Where did she go?"

"No, man. She's gone, she passed away this morning."

"What? What the fuck? Are you fucking me?"

"No. I'm sorry. I didn't want to tell you like this, but I thought you needed to know. She's gone."

I wasn't awake and I didn't know what to say. I tried to tell myself that I didn't care. It wasn't like I was going to miss my mom. I hadn't even seen her since the whole "fucking my future sister-in-law and getting kicked out of the house" thing. They didn't care what happened to me when they kicked me out, but I still found myself crying when Rick told me that mom had died.

I didn't think to ask how it had happened. "Thanks for calling me."

"I think you should come by the house. It might be best for the whole family to be together."

"I'll be there."

There really wasn't anything else to say.

When I hung up the phone, I looked at Gilda on the couch next to me. "That was my step-dad. My mom's dead."

Gilda didn't say anything. She wrapped her arms

117

around me and squeezed me while I cried all over her. I felt emotionally detached from the world, but being there with Gilda felt right.

"I need to go," I said.

"Do you need me to go with you?"

I wanted to say yes. "I had better do this on my own. Things can be a little weird with my brother and step-dad. They don't like me very well. I've been an asshole to them."

"I understand. I think I might go visit my dad then. I have some things I need to do in Nashville and I suddenly feel the urge to go see the old man."

"That makes all the sense in the world. Call me when you get back."

"I don't know how long I'll be gone."

"I''ll be here when you get back."

I wanted to ask Gilda where we stood. I wasn't sure if we were an official couple. I didn't know if we were just friends, with benefits. I didn't know what we were and it didn't feel like the time to clear the air about it. It wasn't like there were very many people that could make me feel the way that she did.

My focus needed to be on getting through the day. I was heartbroken about losing my mom, but I was nervous about seeing her family. I was surprised that they even called me. Things hadn't gone so well the last time I saw them.

I'm sure my brother Joey wouldn't have fucked things up the way I did.

19

When I moved home from Nashville, I moved in with my mom and her new family. I didn't want to live with them, and I doubt they wanted me there, but I didn't have anywhere else to go. The whole thing was just one big, happy powder keg that was ready to blow at any moment.

I wasn't thrilled about being compared to my dead brother or my step-brother, Garrett. I wasn't even looking forward to the prospect of having to see Garrett. He was an ignorant prick. While I went to college, he became a grease monkey. He was a clean-cut, t-shirt and jeans kind of dude, with a crew cut. The only good things the guy had going for him were a steady job as a mechanic, and a seriously hot woman named Whitney. I never understood what she saw in him.

Whitney was attractive, but she looked like a bitch. Some people just look like bitches. She was one of those people. She wasn't necessarily a bad person. There was just something about her coy little smile, and black-hole eyes that made her look like a bitch, a sexy, smooth-skinned, supple-breasted bitch.

I had only been staying with them for a few days when Garrett and Whitney announced their engagement. I couldn't be bothered to give a shit, but my mother was ecstatic. She was certain that we all needed to have dinner together to celebrate. She was wrong.

Having all five of us in the same place at the same time was a retarded idea, but my mother, in all of her naive wisdom, decided it needed to happen. The characters were in place. The table was set. The meal was prepared and devoured.

The entire evening was all about my brother, his busty bride-to-be, and their impending wedding.

I just kept my mouth shut while everyone enjoyed a peaceful conversation during the meal and told jokes over dessert, but when my mom broke into old high school football stories about Garrett, I had heard enough. I had to interject before I threw up my meatloaf.

I stood to raise my wine glass. "A toast to Mr. Fantastic!"

"Don't be a dick, Harlow," Garrett replied.

"Dick? That's funny. It reminds me of a very funny story from when Gary first started dating."

"Nobody wants to hear your stupid story. Just sit down and shut up. You're drunk."

"No! You shut the fuck up, and let me tell my story," I insisted. "You see, Gary always want to date a virgin right? He wanted a really naive chick that he could convince that he was the only man in the world with a penis. Well, he found one. I think her name was Jessica or Julie or something."

"Alright, I think we've all heard enough," My step-dad interjected.

"I'm telling a story here, will you people just let me finish? Damn, now I forgot where I was."

The mood in the room changed and everyone who

was smiling or laughing had stopped. The whole house was a pool of tension. My mother even stood up and walked out of the room. Garrett and his old man just glared at me from across the table. It was hard to tell which one wanted to punch my lights out the most.

I could hear my mother in the kitchen. "Joey certainly wouldn't be going on like this if he were still alive. God rest his soul."

I was actually just about to walk out, when Whitney, of all people, reminded me where I was in my story. "You were saying something about Garrett telling his old girlfriend he was the only man with a dick."

"Right! Thank you, Whitney. At least someone here wants to hear my story," I smiled. "So, he tells her he's the only guy with a dick, and everything is cool. They have sex, she loves it, and she never once thinks about leaving or cheating with another man. Then one day I'm staying over for one reason or another, and I had to take a piss. I mindlessly left the bathroom door open, and this girl just happens to walk by the bathroom, and catches a glimpse of me doing my business."

Before I can finish the joke, my step-dad walks out to find my mom, and Garrett stands up. His fists were clenched in neat little balls of rage and his eyes were burning a target into my face. "Fuck him," I thought, as I sat back in my chair to finish the story.

"The girl goes running into the next room where Gary is watching TV. She's screaming and freaking out and going on. Saying shit like 'I thought you were the only guy who had a penis' and 'you lied to me' and this, that, and the other. Now Gary's been caught in his idiotic lie, and he has to think on his feet, but we know he isn't too bright, so he tells her, 'It's not what you think, I use to have two and since Harlow's my brother, I gave him one.' The girl starts freaking out even more, and yells 'Well...well, why did you have to give him the biggest one!'

As I toss back the last of my wine, you could almost hear crickets chirping.

"The moral of the story is, I got the brains and the cock in this family," I laughed.

I look around the room and see my mom and step-dad standing in the doorway to the kitchen. Whitney had a smug grin, playfully hidden behind her napkin. Garrett doesn't say a word. He looks down at Whitney and at her smile. His wheels turn for a moment before he launches himself across the table, swinging wildly at my face with a grease-stained fist.

His haphazard punch missed me, but he landed unceremoniously in my lap, knocking me backwards out of my chair. We both landed in a pile on the floor. I got up first and waited for Garrett to take another swing. He struggled to stand on wobbly legs.

Garrett stumbled toward me in a 1930's boxer-like pose, but my step-dad stepped between us. "I think it's time to call it a night, and let you boys sleep this bullshit off."

There wasn't really any arguing with Rick since he had kicked both of our asses since we were just kids. He never beat us or even spanked us. His idea of punishment was a couple sets of boxing gloves and a section of the garage blocked off with saw horses. It gave new meaning to going to the corner. Any time Rick though we were getting "too big for our britches," he'd say, "If you're ready to be the man of the house go get in the corner." He called it "The Rincon." He also whipped my ass more than a dozen times. Garrett never even tested him. They just played around and the old man genuinely tried to teach Gary how to box. It was just the way of things with Garrett and me.

I had never asked for shit, but they kept Garrett latched to the tit his whole life. They fronted him the money for him to open his garage, and even moved a trailer into the back yard for him and his bride-to-be. The only thing I'd asked for in my adult life was a place to crash, when my life went to shit.

Thinking about it all made me want to take a swing at all of them, but that was pointless. Whitney and mom helped Garrett off to bed, but dear ole step-dad just stood there looking at me like a failed abortion. "I think, if you don't have any respect for anybody but yourself, you need to pack your stuff and get out as soon as possible," he said with disgust.

"I'm sorry you're under the mistaken impression that I respect myself."

The old bastard didn't say anything else, he just walked away. 'Fuck him,' I thought, as I walked upstairs to take a shower.

As I stepped out of the shower, Whitney came slinking through the bathroom door.

"What the fuck are doing in here? I'm taking a shower."

"Actually, you're getting out of the shower," she smirked.

"It might be a good idea if you gave me a few minutes. You'd be pissed if I walked in on you in the shower."

"What makes you think I wouldn't love the idea of you joining me in the shower? Maybe, I need to see if the story you told tonight is true, at least one part of it...one big part...ever think of that?"

"Whitney, I'm not going to pretend that using your body like a sexy Slip N' Slide doesn't sound more fun than masturbating with a winning lottery ticket, but you're my brother's fianceé. Fuck that."

"Ouch!" She pouted. "That sure tastes like rejection."

"I don't care how it tastes," I protested.

I wrapped a towel around myself and turned to walk out of the steamy bathroom. And that was when I knew my protests had fallen on deaf ears. A pair of hands moved around my waist and cradled my cock. It felt good. It felt real good, and without thinking I turned to face my caresser.

As strong as I am, I am still only a man, and Whitney knew what she was doing with her hands. In a few seconds, I had forgotten she was my soon-to-be-sister-in-law, and my favorite appendage was pointing at the ceiling. She noticed, and as soon as I was ready, Whitney was womanipulating me in her mouth.

I fell back against the bathroom door. She fell to her knees next to me with her lips still locked on me. Sooner than I expected, I expelled the evil from inside, and she was moving up for a kiss.

I met her advancing lips with a deflective hand. "Not so fast, bukake breath. I'm not sure I'm cool with what just happened, but we are sure as hell are not going to seal it with a sloppy kiss."

She cocked her head to the side, with smile. "At least it doesn't taste like rejection."

"Aren't you clever?"

"That's not all I am. I'm also wet."

"I was going to guess, you're also a cheating bitch."

"I've never cheated before. I just wanted to see if your story was true, and now that I know you have the bigger dick, I think I want more."

"That's very sweet of you, Whitney, but this has bad idea written all over it."

"I don't care, and I'm pretty sure you really don't either."

"You are pretty fucking hot and-"

Before I could finish what I was going to say she took my right hand and put it down the front of her already open jeans and under her soft cotton panties, into the soft, warm folds of her vagina.

"So, are we going to do this or not? Everyone else already went to bed."

"I'm not going to lie. Your vagina feels like a very nice place and I'd be a lucky guy to dive in there, but if we go down that road, I have a feeling it only goes to some very dark place."

"I like dark places."

"That's very groovy. I get it but I'm already in a very dark place."

"Good. You don't really have anything to lose then."

"I guess that makes sense, when you put it that way."

"Are going to fuck me or not, Harlow?"

I pretended to think about it, but knew what I wanted to do. I was a slave to my chemicals and a weak creature given to falling into temptation. I really had no choice but to pick her up and awkwardly carry her out of the bathroom, and around the corner to my room. In one magic moment her tank top and jeans were gone, and all of Victoria's Secrets were there on my bed room floor.

As soon as I saw her perky little breasts and well groomed, little heart-shaped bush, I knew I had made a horrible decision, a horribly sexy and worthwhile decision. Just looking at her made me hard, and she was not about to let a hard dick go to waste or give me time to change my mind. She pounced like a hellcat, tackling me onto the bed. It was the kind of raw aggression I had only seen in porno flicks, but she put me where she wanted me, climbed on top of me, and it didn't take long for us to find our rhythm,

Fucking Whitney was a true example of intoxicating sex. It was a form of erotic controlled chaos that we both enjoyed. We enjoyed it so much that we must have forgotten where we were, and ignored how loud we had gotten. It was perfect, until it wasn't.

I was somewhere between getting off and passing out, when I opened my eyes to see Garrett standing in the doorway to the bedroom. I could almost see the gears turning in his head, while he processed what was actually going on, but by the time he had, Whitney and I were both finished.

She didn't notice him at first. It wasn't until she collapsed on the bed that she saw him standing there. She struggled to collect herself, and started apologizing and begging for him to calm down, but I don't think my man fluid dripping out of his future wife was very calming to him.

Garrett cocked his head to the side as I stood to pull my pants up. "Look, I know how bad this looks, and I know you're pissed-" I started, but he wasn't in the mood for words.

He hit me hard enough with one punch to knock me backwards over the bed. As I landed on the other side of the mattress, my head hit the wall, knocking off a picture. The picture landed with a crash on my head. It nearly knocked me out. Disappointed that I was still alive, Gary crawled across the bed and punched me a few more times.

Whitney started crying and screaming for him to stop, but he threw his fist into my face so many times that I lost count. I was defenseless. Blood splattered with every blow, and I couldn't even hold my hands up. Things became a blur after that. The only things I vaguely remember were Whitney running out of the room naked, followed by Rick coming in to pull Garrett off of me.

A couple hours and several wet towels later, I was sitting in the living room bleeding on my mother's beige loveseat, next to Whitney. Across from me on the couch, my brother was wedged between the parents.

"Nothing can undo what has happened here today-" the old man started.

"You're right, Rick," I slurred from behind my busted lips. "I'm a dick and she's a slut. It had to happen. What the fuck are we doing here?"

"If you'll shut up a minute, I'll tell you," Rick yelled before immediately lowering his voice, careful not to excite the volatile situation.

"We think that you need to leave," Mom said. "Whitney is going to move into your room so she's still here. She and Garrett can work out their problems, but I think you owe your brother an apology."

I looked at Whitney. "Really?"

She didn't say anything. She didn't even make eye contact. I couldn't even tell if she wanted to.

"Don't you dare talk to her," Garrett yelled.

I burst into a genuine laugh. "Fuck you! I'm not sorry. All of you can go fuck yourselves!"

After the pussy was out of the bag, I was sure I had destroyed any chance of having a normal relationship with my mom. I didn't care about Rick, Garrett, or Whitney. They were fucking idiots, but I realized I wanted my mom to love me. I wanted her to think something positive about me just once. I didn't want it to be about Garrett or Joey.

It was too late. "Mom, I'm sure Joey wouldn't have fucked Whitney. He's dead. He gets to stay perfect forever. I'm not dead. But thanks for treating me like I am."

I didn't wait for my mom to respond. I wasn't even interested in what she had to say. I just left the house, slamming the door behind me.

Leaving was easy. I didn't have anything to pack or anywhere to go. I would have to dip into my remaining inheritance money. There wasn't much left. I had blown most of it on wine, women, and music, but I had some in the bank for a shitty day.

I was hotel bound.

I hadn't even made it to the bottom of the driveway before I knew what I had to do. I was an asshole. I had to own it and decide how to deal with it. I decided to do the adult thing and get shitty drunk.

20

I wasn't sure if there was a dress code for when a person's mother dies, and nobody told me what to wear. I had plenty of jeans and button-down shirts. I even had the suit I had worn in Destiny's wedding, but I was sure I needed to save that for the funeral. I honestly didn't feel like getting dressed up at all, and I sure as hell didn't feel like facing her family.

There was no getting out of it. I needed to do the right thing and help with the arrangements of my mom's funeral. I wasn't sure if there was going to be any inheritance, or if Garrett, Whitney, and Rick would get it all, but I was sure to be left out if I didn't do the song and dance with the rest of them. It really wasn't about the money to me. I felt like I was owed something for the grief and bullshit I had been dealt. Any money would be nice, but the thing that I couldn't stop thinking about was how I would never get to talk to my mother again. I would never get to be the son she wanted, and I'd never have the relationship with her most sons and mothers have. We had lived my whole life walking circles around each other, only connected by a genetic bond and the hell we put each other through. It wasn't something I'd wish on anyone, except maybe Garrett.

When I got there, everyone was wearing their Sunday best. I didn't know any of the other people walking around the house. I assumed they were from mom's church. They didn't know me, and I looked out of place. I looked sloppy in my Pixies t-shirt and a pair of jeans.

Garrett was the first person I saw. He answered the door, still crying. He was an ugly crier. He was a blubbering, snotty mess. I didn't know how to take it or what to say to him. It was clear to me in that moment how much he loved my mom. She was the only mother he ever really knew, the mother she should have been to me. I hated him for that and he hated me for fucking his wife, but he pulled me in for a hug anyway.

For a moment, I was worried about him getting mucus all over me but I flung one arm around him anyway. I could tell he was hurting. We were both hurting, but it seemed like he was willing to forget all of our previous indiscretions and just be brothers, even for just a day. We could always go back to hating each other when mom was in the ground or wherever.

To make the situation more uncomfortable, Rick joined in on the man-hugging. I wasn't even through the threshold before I was ready to run.

I hadn't been invited to Garrett and Whitney's wedding. It was understandable why, and we had avoided each other at every awkward turn to avoid more drama and chaos. Now, with mom gone, it was all water under the bridge. Bygones were bygones for a while, and then they'd be gone forever because without mom in the picture, I didn't even have a reason to ever talk to Rick, Garrett or Whitney again. That was the thing that gave me the peace of mind to walk through the motions and get past it all.

Dealing with Whitney was the only hard part. It was obvious that Garrett still didn't want us alone together, but those things happen. We did end up alone in the kitchen, and then again while I was smoking a cigarette on the front porch. We didn't really speak much but even with the stench of death still in the air, the sexual tension between us was thick. I hated her and she seemed to be holding some kind of grudge with me, but her eyes gave her away and the thoughts of hate-fucking her on her and Garrett's bed crossed my mind more than once.

Every time I saw her, my sadness went away, and my thoughts were in the gutter, in the gutter having angry sex with Whitney.

The next few days leading up to the funeral felt like I was in a pressure cooker. I could only fake so much happy family fantasy crap. I felt something missing. I wasn't sure if it was a void in my life, or if it was because I wasn't drinking for those days, but it was rough. It was a feeling I wasn't use to, and the tension between Whitney and me was torture. I couldn't stand anything about her, but I couldn't stop thinking about her naked or how hot the sex we had was before Garrett tried to kill me. It was even more crazy because Garrett and Rick were all about us being a family, and letting me know that they were still there for me, as if they had ever been there for me in the past.

They talked about us still getting together for the holidays. Whitney didn't contribute to the bullshit. She stayed out of it. It was probably for the best. I wasn't sure what the best really was. I wasn't even sure if their offers and intentions were serious or if it was just their way of dealing with things. I was less than interested in playing the perfect family, and I was close to telling them what I thought of them on the day we had to say our final farewells to mom.

The funeral was a parade of people I didn't know. None of them knew me either. It was the reason I opted not to stand by the casket shaking hands and hugging strangers. I didn't really care how they knew my mom or how her absence would impact their lives. I almost hated them because most of them probably knew her better than I did.

I was outside smoking and doing pretty well at being standoffish and not being a dick, I thought, until someone wrapped their arms around me from behind. I could tell that it was a woman and she smelled painfully familiar. Her smell was one that I knew but it was slightly off from before. Her scent shot my heart into my throat, and when I noticed the rock on her finger I swallowed my heart back down.

When I turned around, my emotional roller coaster had brought me face to face with Destiny again. I hadn't seen her since her wedding, and I hadn't planned to ever see her again. I assumed she wouldn't want to see me after the ass I had made of myself, but she was there for me, looking only as beautiful as Destiny could. Her was cut the shortest I had ever seen her wear it. It framed her face and emphasized the weight she had gained, but she was still Destiny, and all of the feelings I had been repressing came rushing back.

I had tried not to think about her. I assumed that after her wedding, and how things happened with Elmer, I wouldn't see her again. I should have known better. I should have known that we would find each other again; it was the way we worked. It was something I loved about our relationship, but something was different when she found me at the funeral. I was different.

"You look great."

"Really? Thank you."

"Yeah, really. I've always thought you looked great."

"I know but I cut my hair too short, and I've put on a little weight."

"You look amazing, as usual."

"That means a lot. Thank you. Elmer told me I was getting fat."

I instinctively clenched my fist. I didn't know what to say, but most of the things that crossed my mind involved violence toward her prick husband. He had the perfect woman, and he was too goddamn stupid to appreciate her.

"Wow! What a dick thing to say. He's not exactly skinny himself. What gives him the right to be an asshole to you?"

"He's right. I have gained weight. He's actually lost weight. He's training to be an MMA fighter. I think it's ignorant, but he's in great shape and he's really good. Well, he says he's really good. I don't know."

"Fuck that guy!"

"That's funny. He's not really into that either. He said he only wants to have sex from behind. He doesn't want to see my gut. It disgusts him."

"Motherfucker! Have I mentioned how much I want to punch him in the throat? I still owe him one from your wedding."

"Don't be like that. It's my problem. I got comfortable and gained weight. It happens. I'll drop the weight, and everything will fine."

"He should love you for who you are. He doesn't even know how damn lucky he is."

"He says he loves me. He's just not physically attracted to me. I get it, but he sure loves the hussies at the cage fights. He's all over them."

We walked back into the funeral home for Destiny to pay her respects. I was happy that she did. She understood the tumultuous relationship I had with my mother, but they had always gotten along.

After she gave her condolences to mom's family, we went into an empty room for some privacy to keep talking.

We sat and didn't talk for a little while. I plotted ways to kill Destiny's husband. I don't know what she was thinking about, but it felt like we were friends again. I didn't know what ole Elmer would think of that, and I seriously didn't give a shit. He was a dumb-fuck in need of someone to humble his stupid ass.

The longer we just sat there, the more I realized that I wasn't pissed at Elmer for disrespecting the woman I had loved for most of my life. I was furious with him for disrespecting my best friend of many, many years. I realized that I was finally getting over Destiny. I felt like by rekindling our friendship, I might be able to move on.

Destiny was feeling something completely different.

I was just about to unburden my heart to her again, and come clean about my new platonic feelings, when she leaned over and kissed the side of my mouth. It wasn't anything like the fireworks spectacular I had imagined would happen if she ever kissed me. I had built it up in my head to be an emotional event of orgasmic proportions.

I was shocked and disappointed at my feelings, but she wasn't finished. She assaulted my face with hers again. I liked it, and I hated it at the same time. She jumped across my lap, trying to make out with me like a sex-starved porn star. It didn't feel right on any level. I oddly found myself turned off by her forward approach. It also bothered me that she assumed that she could just attack me like that, and at a funeral. I had waited years for her to make a move, and I had grown tired of waiting. The last thing I wanted was a married version of my dream girl using me to get back at her douche-bag husband, or using me to scratch an itch.

The whole thing felt cheap and unnatural. I knew the feeling well. It wasn't genuine. It was too late to take it all back, but I didn't want to stop her. A big part of me thought that if I let it go on that it might start to feel right. My brain told me that getting physically involved with Destiny would make her resent me for playing a role in her cheating on her husband.

I thought about stopping her, but I remembered how she had made me wait. I thought about how big of an idiot her husband was. I convinced myself that he was probably cheating on her too. I had waited to touch Destiny's naked body for most of my life. If she wanted it to happen, I wasn't about to grow a pair of morals in the heat of the moment. I thought, fuck her husband and fuck her, so I did.

The sex was rough and emotionless. It was nothing like I had dreamed about for years. I tried to take control and live out my fantasy, too, but she was only interested in getting fucked by the bad boy she didn't marry. She wanted me to be rough. She treated me like I was a stranger she had met in a bar, ignoring the fact that I had poured my heart out to her in the past. She ignored the fact that I told her I loved her. To her I was just a tool to get her rocks off, and she knew I couldn't tell her no.

"Baby, pull my hair," Destiny whispered, "I want you to spank me!"

"What?"

"You know how bad we've both wanted this. Fuck me! I want you to pull my hair!"

I reached for a handful of Destiny's hair, but I let go, pulled out, and got up. I had done some pretty fucked up things in my day, but I wasn't going to mess up the one thing I hung onto for most of my life. I didn't want her the way things were. I would rather settle for her as a friend than as the woman I was inside of.

She was only using me, but I wanted to be loved by

her. I had enough of a mess in my life and I didn't need to confuse myself anymore. Destiny wasn't just some woman I went home with from a bar. At one time she was my perfect woman, and I wasn't going to cheapen that for anything.

"What? Why'd you stop?"

"I can't believe I'm going to say this, but I can't do this, not like this. I have wanted to share orgasms with you as long as I've known what an orgasm is, but it can't be like this," I said. "If we're going to be together like this, I want it to be about love. I want to make love to you, not fuck you like some hussy from a strip joint."

"Did you just call me a hussy from a strip joint?"

"No! You know what I mean. I once told you that I loved you, and a lot of things have changed since then. I do still love you, but I can't let you use me, and then run home to your idiot husband. If we're going to do this, let's do it right. Let's be together."

"Wow! I'm shocked," She gasped. "I don't know what to say. I'm sorry. You know we can't be together, Harlow. I'm married."

"That's bullshit. You may be married, but you don't love him or you wouldn't be here with me now."

"You've got it twisted. I do love him. I'm not going to leave him for you. We've had this conversation. I care a lot about you, Harlow, but I love my husband and as long as he's alive, my place is with him. I can't be with you."

I felt more like I was going to cry than I did when I heard about Jack or my mom dying. I'm not sure what came over me, but I decided that Destiny had fucked me and my life up long enough. She wasn't even the person I grew up loving. She was someone else. She was a fat, crazy version of Destiny, and I decided that I didn't need to waste my life anymore on any form of Destiny.

"You need to go."

I couldn't believe the words that spilled from my face. I had never been so stern with her before. I never thought those words would ever be pointed in her direction, but her dumbfounded reaction made my next words even more sharp.

"I don't even know you right now, but I think whoever you are has fucked with me for the last time. Get the fuck out of here and out of my life. You need to get your shit together if you ever want to find your way back into my life, you spoiled, self-entitled bitch!"

Destiny's words that she had said on me, the night of her wedding, came spewing out of my mouth, turned back on her. I directed all the years of my pent-up frustration at her. I wanted her to feel how I felt while she rejected me all those years, confining me to 'friend status.'

She started to cry and I didn't care. "How dare you talk to-"

"I said, get the fuck out of my house!"

When she got dressed and ran out the door, I didn't feel a thing. I didn't feel justified. I didn't feel sad, and I sure as hell didn't feel happy. She had used me, on the night of my mom's funeral, for her own fucked up agenda. That may not have been exactly how it went down, but it was how I felt, and suddenly I didn't feel anything about her anymore.

Butterflies in the stomach replaced with a swarm of arthropods.

Destiny had really worked me up in more ways than one. I wanted to have sex with her. I had thought about it more times than I could count, but I didn't want it to be the way she had come at me.

I had wanted to make love to her and spend the rest of my life with her. She had fucked that all up. I knew I didn't have much of a life to offer her, and I wasn't too good to be used by her, but I was so tired of letting her hurt me.

I could have had sex with her, just for the sex, but I was capable of doing that with anyone. Destiny wasn't just anyone to me. I was even capable of handling things myself, and after as worked up as Destiny had me I was ready to duck into a bathroom and handle it myself. It wasn't the first time I had jerked off to how I imagined sex with her would be. The only difference was that this time I had something more to go on. I had actually seen her naked, and felt her warmth around my cock.

I excused myself to the bathroom, but I had only gotten my dick out when Whitney walked in.

At first, I thought she had just walked in by mistake, but she knew what she was doing. I couldn't understand how she could pull the same shit twice. It had caused us both enough headache the first time.

I knew that hooking up again with Whitney was a terrible idea, but some mistakes were just too fun to only make once.

21

Some mistakes should only be made once. It amazes me that there is even the option to make some twice. I have done some pretty dumb and embarrassing things. Fucking Whitney is one of the worst, but nothing was more embarrassing than the first time I tried LSD.

I didn't fall too far down the rabbit hole of drugs. I usually stuck with alcohol and pot. I felt like I knew what I was getting myself into with those. The only time I did any other experimenting was when Dara and I were together. That was when I tripped acid for the first time. It was nothing like I thought it was going to be. It was marvelous at first, but took an unforgettable turn.

Dara placed the little square tablet on my tongue and told me to relax. I tried, but relaxing seemed like the hardest thing in the world to do. I was terrified that the LSD was going to kick in like something out of a horror movie, and leave me a drooling mess, at the mercy of some weird demons that were really just the living room furniture.

Her way of relaxing me was taking off her shirt. It

didn't relax me, but when she put my hands on her tits, I stopped thinking about the drug entering my system. By the time she had her tongue in my mouth, the trip had begun, and I was putty in her hands. My skin felt alive and it felt incredible.

Once we were heavy into the trip, Dara took my shirt off and drew all over my chest and stomach with a sharpie marker. I just stared at her perfect tits and listened to her talk. Dara talked incessantly about Jim Morrison and not looking into the dark, but in true human nature I took my eyes off of her breasts, and looked directly into the pitch darkness.

Nothing happened, at least nothing that I noticed at the moment.

Being naked was such a beautifully vulnerable thing. My hands naturally moved to cover my junk. It wasn't a perverted thing. It was a safety and a comfort thing. I didn't even notice that I was moving my hands, or that I was hard, until Dara pointed it out. She was wet and excited to try to fuck my brains out. I wasn't sure about doing acid and having sex at the same time. It seemed like a crazy idea. I was afraid of how it would go, and I was sure it was my own paranoia that led to a bad trip. I was also afraid someone was going to get hurt. I wasn't sure how I'd react if I looked down and hallucinated that Dara had turned into goblin, or even worse, if she looked like my grandma.

She assured me that it was all going to be fine. She told me that it was going to be the best sex of my life. Our sex life was already something fit for the Discovery Channel, so I agreed. We were just really getting into things when it got scary. Dara was yelling and moaning like I had never heard a woman moan during sex. I wasn't sure if I was hurting her, or if it just felt that good. I couldn't really feel anything any different. I was also busy looking around the room. I watched her breasts dance all over her chest before I got distracted by the shadows moving on the wall. I knew the LSD had kicked in, and it felt like an exotic free feeling that I couldn't compare to anything.

I was lost in the moment, and closed my eyes to take in the sensation with the rest of my body, but when I opened them I saw Jesus standing next to the bed. He was standing there looking at me like a disappointed parent, but it wasn't the surfer Jesus that most Americans had grown to know and love. It was a strong black Jesus, with hair of black sheep's wool and skin of burnt copper.

I pulled out of Dara, and started freaking out. I knew I was just hallucinating, but even after I blinked a few times and tried to focus, I could still see the beloved son of God standing next to the bed.

Dara said that she couldn't see him. She did her best to calm me down. She held me and kissed my head. She rocked with me until Jesus was gone.

I wasn't sure what I was supposed to take from the whole experience. I wanted to think that I was just tripping, but it felt like a more serious experience. I wasn't sure if I was missing the life-changing message, or if the guilt of my actions had manifested the whole thing, but I couldn't stop shaking.

I felt like a horrible person, and the more she touched me and tried to calm me down, the more awful I felt.

Once Jesus was gone, Dara started laughing at me and tried to make light of the situation. She tried to get me back in the mood. She wanted to get back into the sexy swing of things but when she pulled my mouth to meet hers, I couldn't kiss back. Instead, I puked in her mouth.

She instantly started gagging, spitting, and eventually throwing up. I was so embarrassed that I didn't try to apologize. I was reminded of the shame I felt when I blew my load in my underwear as a kid, only the shame of puking in a woman's mouth was far worse.

I didn't know what to say. The only thing that I thought about was running for the door. That is what I did, and I didn't stop running until I got to my car and I drove my naked ass all the way home.

22

I felt like shit hooking up with Whitney again. I didn't feel bad about her being my brother's wife. I didn't even feel bad because I had sex with her at my mom's funeral. I only felt bad because I didn't know where Gilda and I stood, and it felt like I was cheating on her. We had never made things official, but we had been sharing smiles and orgasms on a regular basis.

When Gilda called me, I had every intention of telling her about what happened. I wanted to be honest, and I wanted to figure out what we were. I hoped that she would forgive me and we would make a run at a serious relationship. I was an idiot.

She had other plans. I never even got to tell her any of it. She apologized for not being there for me. She had lost her mom and she knew how hard it was. It was clear to her that she needed to be in Nashville. I offered to come down there with her, but she didn't want that.

"I'm not coming back," she said. "I need some time to think, and my dad needs me here. I'll be back to get my stuff though. Maybe we could get together then."

"I'm going to miss you, but I'd like to see you when you're in town."

We promised to call each other all the time. We were lying. I was retarded to think that I could make a 'normal" relationship work, anyway.

I was better off drinking alone and wasting time at the Coyote Club with ladies like Deluxury. I loved strippers because they give you attention, and you can't usually take them home. That is, unless the dancer doesn't live in the same house already.

Instead of sitting around missing Gilda, I took my sorry ass to the club. I mistakenly thought that the attention from random naked women might make me feel better. I didn't think about the trouble I could potentially be getting myself into. I should have known that the Coyote Club was no place for a broken heart and most of my paycheck.

After I ordered my drink, my attention was drawn to the stage and the young lady dancing to Joe Cocker's 'You Can Leave Your Hat On.' It reminded me of my favorite scenes in the movie 9 ½ Weeks. Kim Basinger looked amazing in that film, but the girl on stage was pretty attractive, too.

The dark made it hard to see her well, but the series of flashing and flickering lights showed me just enough that I thought I recognized her. I couldn't recall where I knew her from. It was possible that I'd just seen her at the club before.

The stage made it hard to tell how tall she was, but her long dark hair and face looked extremely familiar. I moved closer to get a better look, as I tried to picture her without the hat, and with a few more clothes on, but I was still drawing a blank.

I watched her finished her set, and when her top came off, for the second song, I was sure I'd never seen her breasts before. She had Marry Poppins tits. They were practically perfect in every way.

She was collecting her money from the stage and ignoring a particularly chatty customer, when she looked in my direction. Her hat, and outfit covered her incredible boobs, but without the hat I remembered where I knew her from. She tilted her head to the side slightly and gave me a double take, as if she recognized me, too.

Sure enough. It was a more naked version of my neighbor, Holly the hottie.

"Harlow!" she yelled as she ran over to give me a bare-chested hug.

It quickly became my favorite type of "bare hug."

"Holly, how the hell are you?"

"I'm good but I go by Destiny around here."

"That's pretty fucked up. Of course you do. Why Destiny?"

"I don't know. I've always liked that name. What man wouldn't be interested in what Destiny has in store for him?"

"That's clever. It's just a little weird. I had a friend named Destiny. I guess we're still friends. It's kind of a long story."

"What are you doing in a place like this?"

"I could ask you the same thing. I usually come to talk to Dee and drink this poor excuse for wine, but I've never seen you here before."

"I just started a couple weeks ago. I came for one amateur night and saw how much a girl can make doing this, and it's been my thing every since."

"I'm not complaining. It's really nice to see you. I've always wondered what you looked like naked, and now that is one of life's great mysteries solved."

"You always wanted to see what I looked like naked?"

"You're hot. Of course I did. I'm not blind. I know a

sexy woman when I see one. Who doesn't want to see a sexy woman in the nude?"

"I thought you had a girlfriend. I have seen a girl leaving your house more than once, unless there were different girls and you're just a player?"

"I'm many things but a 'player' isn't one of them."

"I guess that's why you come here."

"Are you kidding me?" I laughed, "You can't meet nice women in a place like this."

"I'm a nice girl, aren't I?"

"I don't know. We've never really hung out. I can say that this is a whole new side of you, though."

"You haven't seen everything."

"I like a little bit left to the imagination. It makes it more fun when I take the mental image of the naked you home with me later."

"I think I'm flattered. That is a compliment, right?"

"Something like that, but I'd be much more interested in taking you out for a bite to eat or a real drink some time."

"I can't date customers."

"Then I'll never be back."

"What if I want you to?"

"I guess we'd better keep it casual, then. I'd still like to see you outside of this place or just in passing at home."

"That's sweet, but I know you hate my dog, don't you?"

"I do."

"I'm sorry. He's my little buddy. He keeps me sane."

"At least he keeps one of us sane. I'm not a dog person."

"I can tell. I can hear you cursing him all the time. At least, I think it's him you're cursing. It might be me you want to rot in hell."

"Oh, you heard that," I chuckled nervously. "I was talking about the dog. You're okay in my book."

"That's cool. Not everyone likes dogs."

"I might be willing to try to be a dog person for the right reasons."

"Or the right person?"

"I don't know. I suck at the whole dating thing, but I might be interested in giving it a try some day. Would you be interested in a bite to eat some time?"

"I think that sounds nice," She smiled. "Do you have plans tonight?"

"Nothing solid. I could say that the concrete is still drying on any plans I may have. Why? Do you have an idea of something I should be doing?"

"Do you wanna come over to my place when I... get... off?"

"I like this idea. I like it a lot."

I waited around for Holly to finish her shift at the club. I had a few glasses of wine and watched her do her thing. She was actually really good. She was a lot better than Dee. She was flexible, and the crowd loved her.

By the time the club was ready to close, I was pretty drunk. I hated the cheap excuse for wine they served at the Coyote Club, but it did the trick. I was pretty sure Holly was drunk, too. I watched her put the liquor away all night. I even bought her a couple drinks, but so did every other guy in the place. It didn't seem to affect her dancing onstage, but she was a little wobbly when she came staggering out of the dressing room.

"Are you still going to come over?"

"I didn't wait here all night for no reason. I thought we had plans."

"I'm ready to go. You can take that however you want to."

"You're drunk, and I think I like where you're going with this. What's a little casual playtime between neighbors, right?"

"I'm ready to stop talking about it," She smiled. "Are you coming, or just breathing heavy?

At the house-

I learned that Holly was some kind of freak.

I wasn't the kind of guy to go around judging other people's sexual preferences, but some things were just too weird even for me. I didn't think I had any unusual fetishes. It was mostly a matter of opinion, and in my opinion, Holly had some twisted fantasies.

"I want you to rape me."

"What? I can't do that," I said. "What the fuck are you talking about?"

"I want you to pretend that you broke into my apartment, and then you get to have your way with me."

"I don't think I can do that. That's pretty fucked-up. It's really not my thing."

"It'll be fine. You might even like it once we get into it. Just go get a knife from the kitchen and sneak back in here. I'm going to pretend to be asleep."

"This is fucking weird. I can't do this."

"Yes, please! It'll be awesome. Just whatever you do, don't stop. If I say don't do something, that is what I want you to do. If I say don't pull my hair, I mean please, pull my hair. Got it?"

"No, I don't got it. This is dumb and confusing. Is this what you're into? Do other guys dig this shit?"

"I don't know. I've never done it before, but I like the idea of my neighbor breaking into my apartment to rape me. You're my neighbor. It's perfect."

"You put thought into this already?"

"Yeah. I even thought about you when I was thinking about it. I was into you when we met. I didn't think things would ever work out like this, though. Come on! Let's do this, please!"

"I don't know."

"Harlow, I said please."

I reluctantly went back into the kitchen and grabbed a big butcher knife. I had no idea what I was getting myself into. I wasn't at all interested in deviant bedroom games, and I wasn't comfortable with a knife being involved with any sexual experiences. Lorena Bobbit screwed that up for almost every man. It had bad idea written all over it. There was no way a sharp object in bed was a safe idea, but I went along with it anyway.

When I walked into the bedroom with the knife, Holly was in her bed under the covers. The light was still on and I could see her clothes in a pile next to the bed, all but her bra and panties. I had already seen her mostly naked, but thinking about her naked got me hard. I thought I might even be able to get into the whole knife play thing, if it meant doing the dirty with her.

It was all fun and games until Monk started barking at me like the little asshole he was. I tried to ignore him, but as I got closer to the bed he got closer to me. The closer he got to me, the more annoying he got with his yapping and freaking out.

"Shut up, Monk," Holly yelled from under the blanket. "Shoosh!"

The dog shut up for a minute but as soon as I touched the bed he started going nuts again. My first instinct was to punt the fucker across the room but Holly ordered him to go to his cage. He barked a little more, but to my surprise he toddled out of the room and crawled into his little kennel.

"I'm sorry. Keep going. You should take your pants off. It will make things easier. I'm only wearing my bra and undies."

"This is so fucked-up."

"It's cool. Just jump on the bed and fuck me. I'm going to fight back but put the knife to my throat and make me stop. Tell me to shut up. Then-"

"I got it. I think I can do this, but you are going to have to stop talking. Between the dog being an asshole and you giving an entire script to follow, I don't know if I can stay hard. It's hard to fake-rape someone with a limp dick."

"Fine. Let's go!"

I flicked off the light, and pulled my jeans down. I unbuttoned my shirt and slid my boxers down on the floor. I was glad she didn't make me wear a mask or something over my face. With the light off it was incredibly dark. I didn't know the layout very well and a mask would have made it impossible to navigate the room. I had enough problems stepping out of my clothes and avoiding dog toys.

Nothing is less sneaky or less sexy than stepping on a squeaky bone in the middle of a crazy role-playing scenario.

I reached down to my jeans to pull a condom from my pocket, but when I stood up Holly was giving me a shitty look. "What the fuck are you doing? Rapist don't wear rubbers!"

"What? Yes, they do! Why would they leave that precious DNA behind to help the police catch them?"

"It's my fantasy and I don't want you to wear one. I'm on the pill. You don't have to worry about anything."

"The pill is a good thing, and I know most guys would be very happy to do the deed without wrapping the steed, but it's called protection for a reason. It's your fantasy but it's my dick. I'm wearing the condom."

"Fine, but don't put it on yet. I want you to rub me with your dick while you run the point of the knife all over my body. It'll be hot. Then I want you to put the knife next to my clit and make me suck you off."

"Wow. Is there anything else? I might need to start writing this stuff down."

"Whatever. Can we just do this?"

"I'm beginning to have my doubts."

Once Holly shut up and the dog was out of the room, things were going well. I was careful not to cut her with the knife, but she leaned into it a little. She arched her back and slid down on the bed until the knife was against her throat. It bugged me, so I moved it away and moved it back towards her pelvis.

Her hips moved with each pass of the blade, and I could see her panties getting wet. I was finally starting to feel like I was doing something right, but I put the knife down long enough to pull her undies down. She pretended to kick at me and actually got me in the mouth once, but it didn't hurt bad enough to stop things.

"Don't you dare put that knife anywhere near my pussy," she said.

Following the list of rules she had presented me with I knew that that was my clue to do exactly what she had asked me not to do. She had mentioned wanting the knife against her clit. I was hesitant but obliged her anyway.

She was the worst over-actor I had ever seen. I was really hoping that acting was what she was going to school for. If it was, she still had a long way to go, unless she wanted to be in soap operas or porn.

Her dialog sounded cheesy and rehearsed. "I don't want your dirty dick in my mouth. You can't make me suck it."

I guessed I was supposed to put it in her mouth, but I had a hard time taking the whole thing serious. I could barely stay hard, and I wasn't sure how to keep the knife to her nether-regions and get myself in a position to have my junk in her face. Nothing about her fantasy worked for me. I didn't know how far the fantasy would even go. Part of me was almost afraid the crazy chick might try to bite my dick off.

She worked with me to get things where they

needed to be, but I still wasn't into it, and it was easy to tell. There was nothing sexy about her pretending that she didn't want to give me a blowjob. There was some awkward feeling of rejection, and there wasn't anything about raping a woman I found fun, even if it was fake.

I tried to think about things that would get me hard, but shit was weird. I tried to remember her being naked in the club, or helplessly waiting under the covers. It worked a little, but I thought if I got rid of her bra and I could see her tits again, it might work. I followed her lead and took one swipe with the knife, cutting the bra and causing it to fall from one beautiful breast. I thought she'd like it and it would be something like the fantasy she had in mind.

I was wrong.

"You just cut an $80 bra! It has a clasp, retard," Holly screamed. "Damn it! What the fuck is wrong with you? "

"If you want me to put a knife on your clit," I laughed, "It kinda made it seem like your bra was fair game. You really need to lay out these guidelines."

"Just get out. This sucks. It's nothing like it's supposed to be. I feel so stupid!"

"Calm down. We can still do this thing. I'll buy you a new $80 bra, and everything is cool. Why don't we try it without the knife and see how it goes? Not all is lost. We're still two mildly intoxicated consenting adults."

She pouted for a few minutes. It was cute, but it really wasn't a turn on. It was more annoying that things were such a cluster fuck. I had honestly never had more difficulty in the bedroom in my life. It was why I was a firm believer that bells, whistles, and handcuffs don't make for a better sex life. I had always thought that if a person knew what they were doing there wasn't any need for gimmicks.

"Fine. We can fuck but I want you to do from

behind."

"I can do that. It's not my favorite, but whatever gets your rocks off that doesn't involve a knife or some warped role-playing session."

"Oh! I'm still role playing. I don't actually want to have sex with you. I was all right with it when I was able to pretend you broke in and just had your way with me, but now I'm going to pretend you're Johnny Depp. I can't do that if I'm looking at you. Just fuck me from behind, and let's get this over with."

"I'm not sure I want to. You're kind of weird and fucking rude. I don't need you to throw me a pity fuck. It's not like your magical mystery box holds the meaning of life."

"I'm sorry. You're right. I was being a bitch. I'm just frustrated. I want you to ravage me, Captain Jack!"

"What?"

"Just go with it. I would rather have a Scissorhand-gasm but I'll settle for a drunken pirate fuck."

"This is so fucked-up."

Holly bent over and thrust her ass in the air. "Pillage my booty!"

I thought about leaving her there to handle things herself, but her pussy was a glistening thing of beauty. She wasn't all worn out like some of the woman I had been with. She was clean and tight and wet with anticipation.

Fuck it.

I took offense to her not really wanting to have sex with me, so I wasn't concerned about how good it was for her. I ignored her requests for me to quote Johnny Depp movies and random pirate clichés. I was only interested in pounding away as hard as I could until I exploded inside her.

The only thing that she muttered were sporadic whimpers and single word prayers.

She was digging at the bed and biting her pillow. Her ass was meeting me thrust for thrust. Things were good. We had hit our stride, and I was just about to climax when I felt something warm and wet penetrate my ass cheeks. I thought that it might have just been sweat rolling down my back, but on the second occasion I moved my hand back there to check. I didn't feel anything, but on the third more persistent pass I felt the unmistakable discomfort of a tongue on my asshole.

I swiped at the feeling with my hand, and felt a fuzzy head around my ass. Monk had worked his way out of his cage and decided to give me a rim job. I nudged him off the bed with my foot and kept my focus on Holly. I wasn't interested in his advances, and it was messing up the nice thing we had going.

The little bastard was persistent. And he had his whole nose in my ass before I even noticed he was there. I didn't want to stop fucking Holly until I was finished, but when Monk's tongue touched my brown eye for the fourth time I was pissed all the way off.

"Three's company, dog! Fuck off!"

I picked him up and gently tossed him off the bed like a football. He landed on his feet, but he crumpled to the ground and started whining like a little diva. There was no way I could have hurt the little drama queen, but Holly shoved me off the bed and rushed to his side.

She picked him up off the floor and held him like a baby. It was awkward to watch an attractive naked woman holding a little mutt. She didn't even seem to care about why I had booted him off the bed. She didn't even pay any attention to the little perv licking her nipple while she glared at me. She was too busy focusing her attention on being a crazy bitch in my general direction.

"I can't believe you would do that! He's just a little puppy! You are a mean, mean man!"

"That little creep was licking my asshole while we were having sex. I'm not into that kind of shit. I was just getting him off the bed. He's fine."

"He's my little buddy. He'll be here for me forever. You're just a casual fuck. I think you need to get the hell out of my house!'

"That's the best idea I've heard all night. You're a crazy bitch. You and that little bastard deserve each other. Maybe you can dress him up like a pirate and let him lick your ass, you freak!"

Holly grabbed my clothes and started throwing them at me. "Don't act like you didn't like it!"

I didn't like it, but I wasn't going to argue with an idiot. She was too busy talking to her dog anyway. I didn't even bother to put my clothes on. I pulled my boxers up and stepped into my shoes before I stormed out of the house. I just trudged up the stairs to my apartment and got in the shower.

Holly avoided me after our drunken knife night. Our almost one night stand left things weird. I still saw her coming and going from time to time, but she didn't speak to me. She nodded and acknowledged my presence. She wasn't a bitch about it, but it was clear we weren't going to be friends or anything else.

I guess the only really good thing that came from our encounter was that she stopped singing all the time, and I never heard her yelling again for Monk to come back inside. He still went out, but it was obvious she didn't want to disturb me. It might have been because she regretted how thing went down, but I assumed it was because she didn't want any reason to have to talk to me.

23

It was my experience that people were into some really weird things, sexually. It was really a matter of opinion, because some things that I considered fucked-up were completely normal to other folks. I'm also sure that things I like, but never had the balls to ask a woman to do, were weird as shit to other people.

Holly the hottie was one of the more crazy ladies that I had ever dipped my dick in, but I considered Dara a pretty odd duck, too. She had a thing for public bathrooms. I didn't understand it, and I never went along with it. It just wasn't something I was into.

Part of being a janitor was knowing just how gross a bathroom really was. I wanted to clean the bathroom at most of the bars I went to before I could take a piss. I understood that a clean crapper didn't make or break the sales in a bar, but I hated pissing in a toilet that wouldn't flush. The hard yellow piss from the patrons before me was always stirred by my own urination. The only thing worse was piss on a massive turd that just wouldn't flush. I avoided them if I could, but sometimes I was doomed to face the foulest stench a bar could produce.

The bathroom at the Seal Club was so filthy I didn't even want to touch myself. The urinal had a better goatee than I did, and it was so low to the ground I felt like I was pissing on the floor. The back-splash usually hit my shoes. I didn't even fuck with the shit station. There wasn't a seat, and it always smelled the way I imagined a gay porn set would smell.

The weird part was that I actually preferred a filthy bathroom to one of those bathrooms that have automatic lights, automatic flush toilets, motion-censored sinks, and even electric paper towel dispensers. Fancy, modern restrooms made me feel dirty for doing my duty. The only nice thing about clean, robo-bathrooms were that they were the only restrooms I'd ever consider having sex in. I have never been one for getting in public restrooms, but Dara was all about it.

The first time that she followed me into the bathroom, I freaked out and told her to leave. I had just taken a leak, and she was ready to give me head in the stall. I loved head as much as the next guy, but dirty-dick head, in a dirty stall, seemed like a mysterious infection waiting to happen. I wanted to wait until we got back to her apartment, but she didn't see the adventure in that.

I didn't see the adventure in getting frisky in a nasty bathroom. It seemed more like Russian roulette or dodge the STD to me.

Dara got that I wasn't into bathroom games, but she still tried her luck when we were together. The most fucked-up attempt was when she wanted to give me head one night at the Pour House when I was brave enough to take a shit in the filthy bathroom. Nothing sounded appealing about have my dick sucked while I was taking a shit, to me. She assured me that it would be cool, but it never happened.

She once told me that anal sex felt like taking a really good shit over and over again. She also told me that guys could get off from stimulation of the prostate, but I wasn't interested in that action or engaging in anal or bathroom sex. The closest we ever came to doing what she kept begging for was me going down on her in a Cheesecake Factory bathroom.

"I could give you a hand job. That might get you hard and make you think differently about public restroom sex, huh?"

"I don't think so. I'm not really a big hand job guy any way. Why would I need you to give me a hand job?"

"Because it would feel good, stupid."

"I know it feels good. I've been giving myself hand jobs for years. That's pretty much what jacking off is."

"Fine. I'll never touch your dick again. I'm sure you can do just fine without me, asshole!"

"Why are you being like that?" I tried to explain, "I'm just not into that."

"I want a little strange in our relationship. I want to spice things up. I want you to want to do something crazy, with me!"

"We can do all kinds of crazy shit. I just don't need you to give me a hand job in bathroom. I have that covered."

Dara pouted. "That is what I mean. You jack off in the bathroom all the time. Why is it so bad to fuck me like an underage stranger in a public bathroom?"

"I'm not even sure where to start, Dara. There are a lot of things so ridiculously wrong with what you just said."

The end result of all this wrangling about sex and toilets was that I thought about Dara a lot when I used public bathrooms. I'm sure that was her goal, that and to get off. At the end of the day, we're all just trying to get off.

24

I felt lost without Gilda around. I had gotten used to having someone to eat and sleep with. I was used to having somewhere else to stay. After the bullshit with Holly, and my car being trashed, I wanted to be anywhere but my apartment.

Without my car, I was limited to the places I could walk to. That only left a few bars, my neighborhood Save-A-Dime, and a handful of restaurants. I wasn't willing to walk very far. It was too much like exercise, and I didn't like to sweat or juggle unless there was an orgasm involved.

My laziness and need for a drink led me to try a new bar, one that was close enough to walk to. I usually avoided sports bars, but I was lured in by a "FREE BEER" sign. I was will to suffer through whatever they called entertainment for free drinks. I had no idea what I was actually getting myself into.

The FREE BEER came after a $10 cover charge. It was all you could drink, so it still seemed like it might have been worth it, until I saw that it was a nasty local

IPA, which they served in tiny little plastic cups. That really wasn't worth messing around with. I would have left in disgust, but the spotlight event of the evening was a wet t-shirt contest, and the bar made up for the shitty beer with FREE JELLO SHOTS.

I didn't like Jell-O or vodka, but I liked being drunk, and I had never been to a wet t-shirt contest.

I had always thought that it would just be a bunch of dude-bros being sexually crass to women with nice tits and ton of self-esteem issues. My perception was pretty accurate. The only thing I didn't count on was for the girls to get as crazy as they did. They were getting fully naked and booty dancing all over the bar. It was like I had stumbled into a Girls Gone Wild: Spring Break Special, and after a bunch of Jell-O shots, I was loving every minute of it.

It was all fun and boobs, until the vodka hit me. It like an angry drunk step-dad. I hadn't kept track of how much I was drinking, and before I could hit a good stopping point, I was falling all over the place and jabbering to anyone who would listen. I was going on and on about Gilda and Destiny, and how unhappy I was. I wasn't myself. I had become the annoying drunk guy. It wasn't the first time, but it was the first time I that I noticed I had made a drunk ass out of myself in front of a whole group of total strangers.

The bouncer was pretty cool about the whole thing. He offered to call me a cab, but I lied and said that I just lived around the block. I didn't really remember how far away I lived, but I let him walk me out. I didn't walk very well without him holding me up, as hard as I tried to walk like I was cool. The best part was telling everyone I passed on the sidewalk that I wasn't drunk.

My apartment really was only a couple blocks away, but I went in the opposite direction, lured by a Denny's sign glowing in the distance. Going to get food seemed like the only thing to do at that point. There were several restaurants around me, but I just had to stagger my drunken ass the four blocks to Denny's. It wasn't my smartest idea. A smarter guy would have avoided the chances of getting picked up for public intoxication and just gone home, but Denny's was like a second home for my friends and me, back in the day.

I stumbled into the greasy eatery, and immediately my eyes were drawn to a table of chubby cops. I tried to look as sober as possible, something I'm sure I didn't do well. I expected them to arrest me every time they looked my way, but they were more interested in their cannibalistic feast of bacon and sausage.

The lizard-looking woman behind the counter led me to a booth that was too close to the cops for my dining comfort. I pretended they weren't there, and focused on the menu. I knew I needed food in my system as fast as possible, but I didn't know what I wanted. Everything looked good through my blurry eyes.

I eventually just pointed to a yellow and brown blur on the menu, and I ordered a glass of grapefruit juice to wash it down. I didn't know exactly what I ordered, but I wasn't worried about it. I willing to eat anything. As soon as I placed my order, my eyes fell shut and I passed out in the booth.

I don't know how long I was passed out, but when I woke up, my food was on the table in front of me and the cops were gone.

I could feel everyone watching me, and the room was still spinning. I realized in no way was I fit to be in public. I figured that my only chance of survival was to sleep it off. I didn't waste time eating my food. I just slumped over the table, and felt the room spin, until I worked up the motivation to leave.

The next morning, I woke up covered in sweat,

naked, in the middle of a king-size bed. I was in a scorching hotel room. I was alone, at least when I woke up. I wasn't even sure if I had rented the room or just broken in.

As I rolled off of the bed, I continued to search for my clothes and memories of the previous night. I didn't know why I stayed in the hotel. I didn't like hotels. I'd had a problem with them after Jack died. They all looked the same to me, and I imagined Jack waiting for me in the bathtub.

My clothes were the only things that were easy to find. They were spread out on the bathroom floor like a chalk outline, as if I'd placed them there in the shape of me. The entire bathroom was a mess that included an ice bucket in the toilet, and a sink full of shampoo, conditioner, and a few other things. I had dumped them all in the sink and left the bathtub full of cold water that was as murky as my memory.

I knew I had to get the fuck out of there. The heater was turned all the way up, and I didn't know how to turn it down. I wasn't sure if I was even the one who turned it up. I wasn't sure of much other than the fact that my whole body hurt and my head was pounding. It felt like it weighed twice as much as usual.

As I left the hotel, I noticed that the Denny's from the night before was next door, and some things started coming back to me. The cooking food from the restaurant smelled good, and I thought about getting something to settle my stomach. I was pretty sure there wouldn't be anyone working now who might have been there the night before, but I wasn't positive, so I decided to pick another place to eat. I really only liked Denny's when I was drunk. I didn't mind the food, but the memories were hard to stomach. It was a greasy reminder of better times.

25

Jack, Nathan, and I had some pretty interesting times at Denny's. It was our hangout for a while when we were in high school. We even had our own booth. My favorite Denny's experience was one of Nathan's most embarrassing moments. It was before he started dating Abigail, and before everything went to hell.

He wanted to go with Jack and me to meet up with my girlfriend at the time, Marilyn, and her best friend, Beth. We called Beth the record store girl, because she worked at the music store, and she wouldn't tell us her name for the longest time. We did it because she didn't like it. It was what immature guys do.

Nathan liked the record store girl. She liked Jack. The girls had asked Jack and me to meet for coffee. Jack wasn't interested, but the girls and I agreed to meet up, and they allowed Nathan to come along, to see if he and Beth would hit it off.

Being the macho man he was, Nathan decided to start slamming back Wild Turkey as soon as we made plans to meet at Denny's. I think he was drinking his courage to chat up Beth. He was too shy otherwise, but by the time we picked him up the bottle was empty, and he looked like he already regretted his decision. A fifth of whiskey in twenty minutes is never a good idea, especially since Nathan was not a heavy drinker. He was more of a cheap beer kind of guy.

The whole car ride to dinner he just kept mumbling "I'm gonna puke."

Jack and I offered to take him home, but he was not about to miss a semi-date with record store girl. He just choked it back and made his way into the restaurant. We all placed our orders, and before Nathan could take one drink of coffee, he passed out face down on the table.

Our waitress was a heavy chick named Debbie. She reminded me of Rosie O'Donnell in her more plump years, but she was very, very nice. She kept coming by and asking if Nathan was all right. We didn't know.

"Yeah, he's fine," we said.

We were wrong. Jack seemed annoyed that Nathan had passed out on the table, but it didn't bother me. I figured, he made his drink, he could swim in it. The rest of us were having fun, drinking coffee and talking about what celebrities we wanted to sleep with.

Then, as if God had slapped him upside the head, Nathan sat up and yelled, "Betty Fuckin' White!"

We all burst into laughter. Nathan didn't laugh. He just looked around, with one eye half open. He knew how stupid he had to look, but as he went to laugh, his body had other plans. An unmistakably panicked look swept over his face as his hands shot up to cover his mouth. This wasted motion came a little too late. Whiskey-scented vomit sprayed between his fingers, hitting every one of us at the table.

"I'm not dealing with this shit," Jack said.

"It's no big deal," Marilyn laughed. "We'll take him home."

It was easy for her to say. She got the least amount of puke on her. I had shielded her with myself. My flannel shirt took most of it. I was covered in barf, but it was still funny as hell to me. All I had to do was take the flannel off, wash my hair out in the bathroom, and it was all good.

Jack and Beth left very abruptly. It was cool to see them leave together, but the circumstances were not what I think anyone wanted.

Nathan was into her, but she and Jack just clicked. It was a relationship based on a love for music, particularly Bob Dylan. They hooked up and dated for a few months, but all they did was listen to records, get high, and have sex. I didn't see Jack much for those months.

Debbie was right there to help Nathan clean up the mess. He was still drunk, but he seemed a little more with it. He was rambling and staring down Debbie's top as she bent over to clean the puke off the floor.

When she was finished, she went to the back to grab the mop. Nathan jabbed me in the ribs. "Holy shit, man, did you see the size of those fucking tits?"

I didn't really know how to react. "What are you talking about? Yeah, she has gigantic boobs, but she also has a huge ass, thighs, and everything else too."

"No way. She's pretty good looking. I think I could nail her, if I tried."

"Nathan, since I am your friend, I'm not going to sugarcoat this for you," I began "I'm pretty sure you are retarded. You are covered in your own vomit, half drunk, and this bitch looks like Brunhilda the Sumo wrestler, but what the hell? Go for it."

When Heavy Debbie came back with the mop and a fresh cup of coffee, Nathan set his plan in motion. Before too long, she was rubbing his back and telling him, "Everything is going to be all right."

I thought I was going to be sick, too.

Debbie said her shift was about over and that she'd be happy to give Nathan a ride home, if the rest of us wanted to head home and get cleaned up. I thought it was a bad idea, but Nathan was dead set on making sweet love to our super-sized server. He told us to go. I gave him one more look of doubt as we walked out the door. He didn't come running out after us.

When Marilyn and I got back to my house and got changed, we argued over what movie we were going to watch. Nothing sounded good to me, and we ended up chilling on my bed, channel surfing and talking

Marilyn was worried about my mom being home, but I was just getting her warmed up to the idea of getting frisky, when my phone rang. I did my best to ignore it, but it's next to impossible to get a girl in the mood with the phone blaring next to the bed. I knew without even answering it, it was Nathan.

My first reaction was: Fuck him. He can deal with whatever he's got himself into. But just as my curiosity was just about to get the best of me, the phone stopped ringing and my mom yelled that it was for me. I pretended that I didn't hear her, but when she yelled the second time, Marilyn handed me the phone.

"Just see what he wants, he might really need help and you did kind of just leave him high and dry."

"Fine, but he probably just sobered up and figured out what was going on, "I said.

On the other end Nathan was in a panic."Goddamn it, man, get over here and pick me up!"

"Oh, what's wrong, Romeo? Is your sumo wrestling match a little too much for you to handle?"

"Shut up and get over here, now!"

Nathan was in no mood for jokes and he sounded like he was shitting bricks. He gave me her address and hung up the phone before I could even get another wisecrack in. I would have rather stayed in bed with Marilyn, but I was really curious about what he had gotten himself into.

Marilyn wasn't up for any more adventure, so she said she was just going to go home.

I found Debbie's house, and Nathan was already standing outside waiting for me. He jumped in the car and didn't say a word, all the way back to his house. He lived on the other side of town and no matter what I asked, he just stared out the window, like he had seen a ghost.

"So what the fuck happened? Did you puke on her?"

Nothing.

"Did her angry husband come home early from work?"

Nothing.

Then finally as he was getting out of the car I asked, "Did she have a bunch of body parts and half eaten people in her fridge or something? Damn it. Don't leave me hanging," I said. "I passed up getting laid to pick your sorry ass up. You freakin' owe me."

He sat back down in the car and looked me deep in the eyes. "I'll tell you, but if you ever tell another living soul, I swear to God, I'll kill you."

"So what is it?"

"You have to swear. This is by far the most embarrassing and disgusting thing that has ever happened to me in my life."

"Damn, this must be some freaky shit. Okay, I swear. I won't tell."

"So, me and that big girl started messing around and I was playing with her tits. It was like I was in a sea of boobs," he said. "She started giving me a hand job, while I tried fit one of those massive breast in my mouth. Then she asked me to titty-fuck her."

He paused for a minute, before he turned his attention back out the window. I could tell he was being forced to relive whatever had just happened.

"It was pretty dark in there, so I grabbed two big ole handfuls and started fucking like a wild man. That was when she screamed 'what the hell are you doing?' I was so into it, I yelled back 'I'm fuckin' these titties!' The next thing I know she hits the light, and I see that I have a tit in one hand, and half her gut rolled up in the other hand."

I didn't need to hear anymore. I was laughing so hard that my chest hurt. He didn't see the humor. He just got out of the car and flipped me off.

Of course, I told everyone.

I though it was funny. Everyone else did, too. He got pissed when I told everyone, and he got mad any time someone brought it up. He never actually tried to kill me, he was just a dick to me after that.

26

I was upset when Nathan had moved away. I was even more sad that he didn't bother to come back for Jack's funeral. He and Abby sent flowers, but I was sure that was Abby's idea.

When Jack was going through his hardest times, Nathan wasn't there. He was too busy. He was in Chicago, and he turned his back on his friends. He was a real sonofabitch, but I didn't know how big of a piece of shit he was until I finally talked to Abby again.

My janitorial night job still had me cleaning the public library, but I made the best of it.

I started looking at different books to pass the time. I found a few authors I really liked, but I got to the point where I was reading everything I could. I just enjoyed reading. It was a good escape from being me.

I started with Charles Bukowski. Gilda had told me that I would like his stuff, so I looked him up. She also suggested Jack Kerouac. He was my stepping-stone into my addiction to the beats, and before long, I was also hooked on other authors like Ray Bradbury and Kurt

Vonnegut, too.

One night while I was cleaning, I noticed that the library had scheduled an appearance by Author Abigail White. She was going to be in town during Memorial Day weekend, signing copies of her paranormal romance series. I wasn't into that genre of book, but I knew the author's name very well.

I was so pissed at Nathan for missing Jack's funeral that I had lost touch with Abby, too. I didn't even know that she had received a publishing deal, and a chance to tour with her books. I also didn't know that she and Nathan had split up. They dated through most of high school and a few years after. The two of them moved to Chicago, got married, and were living happily ever after, until she caught him bumping uglies with a barley legal, barista.

Abby kept the condo, a nice monetary settlement and their two dogs, Drake and Bella. Nathan got the Hybrid SUV, the remaining payments, and the coffee-shop girl's Chlamydia. Abby made out like a buxom bandit, and he got everything he deserved.

It couldn't have happened to a nicer guy.

I had secretly always had a little thing for Abby, but Nathan and she were an item, and our other guy friends droned on about "if they ever split up", so I did what any mature person would do, and I hid my admiration behind a wall of sarcasm, ridicule, and other bullshit. I wanted it to seem like I couldn't stand her, and was in no way interested in seeing her naked and exhausted on my bed.

It worked even better than I anticipated. Even Abby thought I hated her.

So, knowing that Abby would be in the area, I bought a couple of her books and read them, well, one of them. It was pretty hot stuff. I wasn't into the vampire and werewolf romance garbage, but I really enjoyed the sex scenes. They were detailed to the last drop.

I tried not to, but I couldn't stop imagining Abby in the female lead role. It was easy since the female lead was a busty, raven-haired beauty, with breathtaking blue eyes, like Abby. I skipped the description of the heroic wolf-man, the love interest. I pictured myself as the beast ravaging her between the sheets.

The night of the book signing, she was surprised to see me standing in her line. I had brought one of the books I had bought. I didn't really need her autograph, but I let her sign it anyway. I could always say that I knew the author before she was famous.

There wasn't anyone in line behind me, so I read what she wrote.

She signed it -

To my favorite asshole:

Thanks for the support. We should get a drink sometime.

Love,
Abigail White

I liked the idea of getting a drink and catching up. She didn't draw a very big crowd, and I didn't know the etiquette for a book signing. I was just going to leave, but she made some small talk.

"How are ya?"

"I'm good, and when I'm not, I fake it well."

"I understand faking it."

"I've heard that most women do."

"Ever the asshole, huh?"

"Not really. I've calmed down a lot. I'm more focused on destroying myself than I am making other people miserable."

"Nice! I'm sure you deserve some of it, but don't be

too hard on yourself."

"Yeah?"

"Yep. That's my job. I think I still owe you."

There was a pause while I read her inscription on the inside of my book again. She fidgeted with her pen. It was clear that neither one of us knew what to say to the other. It made me regret several years of being a jerk to her.

"I should go. I don't want to hold up the line."

"I think there's only twelve people here. You're fine."

"You have a point."

"You should stay. I'm going to read something from my next book."

"I might stick around, but we should definitely get a drink and catch up. That's a good idea."

It was weird to be in the library when it was open, but I stayed to watch her read. I kept thinking that someone was going to say something to me about the books I had been reading and taking home, without permission, but nobody said anything, and by the time Abby started reading, I had forgotten all about my criminal reading indiscretions.

She read a couple chapters of her unpublished works, and it seemed like she was looking right at me when she was reading the start of a steamy sex scene. She stopped right before it got to the good part, but I felt like she was smiling at me. She might have even been a little embarrassed that I was there, but after reading some of it on my own, it turned me on a little.

After she finished reading and talking to her readers, she asked me if I had plans.

"Do you have plans? I was thinking we could get that drink we talked about."

"That sounds great. I know a cool little place, with a good wine selection."

"You can have the wine. You should know, I'm a whiskey girl."

"I don't know how that slipped my mind. That seems like the sort of thing I'd recall, but I can show you to a great whiskey bar. It's not far."

"I need a drink after doing these author things. Lead the way!"

I didn't really know of a good whiskey bar, but I assumed that The Seal Club had good whiskey. All of the metal kids drank the hard stuff. I had learned my lesson, and I stuck to wine. Abby drank the hard stuff.

Talking to Abby meant that Nathan would eventually come up in conversation. I didn't really want to talk about him. I doubt Abby did either, but it didn't take long for him to pop up.

Abby swallowed her first drink in one gulp."Do you ever talk to Nathan?"

"I think I saw him for a second at Destiny's wedding, but he didn't speak to me. He probably knew how much I wanted to hit him in his mouth," I said. "Once you guys moved to Chicago, he wasn't really very interested in hanging out with Jack and me. He didn't even come back for Jack's funeral. That surprised me. I expected to see both of you there."

Abby hung her head. "I'm really sorry about that, Harlow. I know how close you and Jack were. I think Nathan was jealous sometimes. I wanted to go to the funeral, but Nathan was dead set against it. He didn't like the way things went down. He thought it was bullshit that Jack killed himself.

"That's bullshit. Nathan should have been there. Jack never did anything wrong to Nathan. He was always a good friend. I didn't like the fact that he killed himself either, but he was my best friend. He was Nathan's friend, too."

"Nathan kept telling me that suicides go to Hell. I

173

don't know if I believe that, but he said that Jack made his choice. He chose death over everything, and everyone. I think Nathan even blamed you for part of what happened to Jack."

"Fuck him! He was so high and mighty, he didn't do anything to help. I was there. I helped keep Jack sober for three fucking years!"

"I know, I know!"

Abby pulled me in to give me hug. I felt my eyes well up with tears. I didn't want to cry, but talking to Abby had me really upset. It made me miss Jack more than all the time with Gilda had. It also upset me that Nathan could be so stupid and heartless. If I hadn't already wanted to punch Nathan in the throat, talking to Abby made me want to do it even more.

If he had been standing in front of me, I might have done it, too.

It felt nice to be pressed against Abby. It was the first time, in all of our years of knowing each other, that we had hugged. She was warm, and I could feel her chest pressing against mine. I must have jerked off to a mental image of what her tits looked like a million times when we were younger.

Thinking about Abby's boobs brought me out of my funk. It became the only thing I could think about. Nathan and Jack moved to the back of my mind, and I was focused on the memories of Abby when we were younger, and how damn nice she still looked.

The best part was that I didn't have to be an asshole to her anymore. I could just be myself and see what happened. I was mostly interested in reforming or forging a friendship, but I was also completely open to satisfying my adolescent curiosities, if she was interested in anything more.

"Enough of this heavy shit we can't do anything about," I said. "Look at you following your dream. You always said that you wanted to be the next Stephen King."

"No, I said I wanted to get next in line to bone Stephen King."

"You have a point. That must have been it. My mistake."

"What did you always want to do with your life? I may be a bad friend, but I don't remember you ever mentioning any dreams or goals like that."

"I didn't really think about it too much. I still don't."

"What would you do, if you could have any job you wanted?'

"I don't think anyone wants to work. Not having a job would be the dream job, right?"

"True, but what would you do if you didn't work? What would you do for fun?"

"I like drinking. I'd probably do a little more of that. I might eventually get sick of it and settle down, with a pretty lady."

"That doesn't sound very exciting at all. What did you go to school for?"

"I took a lot of journalism and English classes. I think I was trying to stumble into being the next Hunter S. Thompson, but it wasn't for me, and I don't really want to be Thompson. I just wanted to write for Rolling Stone. It would have been cool to travel, see incredible shows, and hear new albums before everyone else."

"You wanted to be a writer, then?"

"I wanted to write about sex, drugs, and rock 'n' roll."

"You still can."

"I don't think Rolling Stone is going to hire me. I've written a few things, but I haven't done much, since Jack died. I haven't felt like it. The music just doesn't sound the same without him."

"That's bullshit. You can still write about all of that

stuff you love. You could write a book. You might even know a published author, willing to give you notes and help you get it published."

"You'd do that for me?"

"That what friends are for. We didn't always get along, but I've always kinda liked you. You were just a total asshole to me all the time."

"I'm sorry about that. I just didn't want anyone, including you, to think that I liked you. You had enough guys swooning over you. I wanted to be different."

"You also only had eyes for Destiny. I didn't think you liked me. I never really thought about what would happen if we hooked up. It didn't seem like it'd ever happen."

"You were right. You and Nathan hooked up and you guys were good, for a while."

"That was then, and we all know how that turned out."

"I'm sorry about that. I never thought that was going to happen. He's a fucker. You can do better that that self-serving prick anyway. Fuck him!"

"I don't think I want to do better. I just want to drink this whiskey and make bad choices. It's my turn."

I looked around the bar. "I can get behind that idea. You're a hot chick. Maybe we could even find you a handsome devil to take you home and help you work out some of that pent-up frustration."

"Are you going to be my pimp?"

"I'm not a very good pimp, but I'll do what I can. My mission tonight is to get you drunk and get you sexed."

Abby rolled her eyes. "You're all heart."

I don't think that she could have been any more sarcastic.

"We can do whatever you want. If you want to just go home alone that's cool, too, but I'll do my best to find you a good guy, or even a girl, if that's what you want."

"We'll see how the night goes. Right now, we need more whiskey."

I lost track of how much we drank. Abby nursed her whiskey. I didn't waste time. I liked to drink my drinks, and the wine went down much smoother. She was more interested in conversation, but the only guy she was talking to was me. It made it hard to live up to my promise to hook her up with a bad decision.

She kept finding things wrong with every guy I pointed out. I tried to tell her that she was missing the concept of making bad choices. I was an old pro. The trick is to not care at all, and to deprive yourself of the person you truly wanted to be with. It was usually pretty easy.

While I was talking to Abby, she pointed out that I had always been pretty good at making bad choices.

"I'm not going to hold you to finding me a one night stand. I think I can handle that on my own. Just do your thing. I'm sure you'll hook up with someone. Isn't that what you do?"

"Yes and no. Jesus, I'm not sure, but that sounded a little harsh. Is that what you think of me?"

"I'm not judging," she said. "I was just giving you a pass."

"Why can't I just hang out with you, and have fun? Why does it have to be about either of us hooking up, or making a bad decision?"

"I just figured you wanted to have more fun and do your thing. It's not like you and I are going to hook up. That would be the ultimate bad decision!"

"What the fuck is wrong with me? There is more to me than getting drunk and screwing things up. You know that, right?"

"You made the choices that have landed you where you are. You have to make the choices to get out of the shit you've buried yourself in."

"No one really taught me how to be an adult. My dad was living in a fantasy world until he ran off to San Francisco, to be a homosexual stereotype, and mom was too busy pretending I didn't exist."

I was getting drunk and emotional. It happened from time to time. I was usually much better at not pouring my heart out to people, but when Gilda left that changed. Seeing Abby again just brought it all out.

I felt like I was feeling sorry for myself, but Abby didn't let me get away with it. "That's the saddest thing I've heard all night. I would feel sorry for you, but you seem to be doing alright. You have a job, good drinks, and a sea of pointless pussy. Life can't be that bad. That's what every guy wants, right?"

"No! That's bullshit. You know I want more than that."

"Then stop making the same stupid choices, and go after what you want."

"I'm not sure what I want."

I could tell Abby was drunk. "I don't either. I think I want another drink."

"I think that might be a bad idea," I assured her.

"Isn't that the point of tonight? Aren't we going to get drunk and make bad choices?"

"You just told me to stop doing that."

"You can stop tomorrow. You're going to be a writer, but tonight I want you to be my bad decision."

I assumed that Abby had misspoke, but the look she was giving me cleared everything up.

We took a cab back to her hotel and started peeling off clothes as soon as we got into her room. She looked even better naked than I imagined. I could tell she worked out, and her boobs were astonishing. They were just the right size, pale and perfect, with the softest nipples I had ever seen. They were the kind of tits that made it hard to look at the rest of her, but I turned my attention to her healthy heart-shaped ass, and the cute little tuft of hair where her legs came together.

I dove into going down on her, but she assured me that it wasn't going to work. I took it as a challenge. After a while I was starting to get tired, and I thought that she might have been telling the truth. I would have continued, but she thanked me and offered to return the favor.

Abby gave the worst head. It was more like she was afraid to touch my dick with her hands or her mouth. It was like she was only doing it to be nice, and it wasn't even nice. I would have just asked her to stop, but in one of my more insulting moments, I fell asleep.

I didn't mean to. It just happened. We never made it past oral sex.

Abby was still asleep when I woke up. She had gotten up, gotten dressed, and come back to bed. She didn't snuggle or anything. She was all the way on the other side of the king-sized bed, careful not to touch me. I imagined she was either extremely regretful of her bad decision, or highly offended that I passed out while she was going down on me. It didn't really matter either way.

It was still dark outside, but I couldn't go back to sleep. I opted to get dressed and sneak out, instead. If Abby woke up as I left, she didn't make any attempt to say anything, or stop me from leaving. It was probably for the best. She had her shit together. The last thing she needed was me in her life to fuck things up.

I'm sure my brother could have got Abby off, stayed awake to get head, and fucked her like a machine, but I was tired of thinking about everything my dead brother could have possibly done better than me. The fact was that he was dead, and I wasn't. I needed to stop playing dead and do something with my sorry self.

I was going to be a writer.

27

Wanting to be a writer, and actually being able to put words on the page are two very different things. I had things I wanted to write about, but I assumed that nobody gave a shit. I had a similar problem when I came back from Nashville.

I was fresh out of college and hiding from my feelings for Gilda. My plan was to move home, keep myself busy with the written word, and make a name for myself as an author. The only thing I hadn't figured out was if I wanted to do fiction or establish myself as a columnist. I figured that there was more money in essays and nonfiction. I wanted to follow the money, and still write about the things I wanted to write about. I wanted Rolling Stone magazine to come knocking on my door. It was a stupid plan, but I thought if I was cool enough, and wrote enough about the things Rolling Stone covered, it would only be a matter of time. I was dead wrong.

I had just moved into my own place, after fucking Whitney, pissing off my family, and getting the boot from home. I planned to write about my life and the fucked-up people I knew. I, like too many others, thought my story mattered, but I learned that when I sat down to write about my adventures, I couldn't even find an interesting way to put it on the page. I beat my head against the typewriter for days before I finally gave up and decided to have a drink.

On the way to the Save-A-Dime store, to buy wine, I stopped for a drink, to take the edge off. I was intimidated by the blank page. I could have just gotten my bottle at the Save-A-Dime, and gone home, but I knew the page would be there waiting for me, so I allowed myself to be lured in by the neon lights of a restaurant in the same strip mall as the liquor store. I didn't like the drink prices, but sometimes a guy just needs to sit on a bar stool and have a drink.

There is something particularly sad about drinking alone in the middle of the day. I felt like this was even more pathetic because I was drinking in a bullshit chain restaurant. I tried to kid myself that I had a little more class. As long as I faced the bottles behind the bar, I could fool myself into thinking I was in a real bar instead of the land of overpriced Mudslides and 2 for $20 deals.

The restaurant bar was full of other sad sacks. They were all drinking for their own reasons. I didn't care what their reasons were. I didn't get involved with any of the other fools in the bar. I just wanted to drink my over-priced wine and hide from my own bullshit.

All of the characters were in place.

There was the cheap suit business man, talking loud enough for everyone in the bar to hear how successful he was. He claimed that he sold cars to celebrities. The only person buying his hot load of crap was the once-attractive woman, sitting between me and the used car salesman. She wasn't even listening. She was just looking for someone to punch her ticket. Everything about her was a mess. She looked the way a beautiful woman would look after week-long crack binge with Lindsey Lohan and Amy Winehouse.

At the other end of the bar, we had the sports fan that was between jobs. He kept his eyes on the various televisions. He was easily identifiable by his backwards baseball cap, representing his team. The guy a few seats away from him was almost as pathetic. He was the middle-aged man with a beer gut, and prominent bald spot. He hated his wife and kids. He was going to do something with his life and be a somebody, until he forgot to pull out one night. He looked at the only good-looking woman in the bar. I didn't have to make up a story for her.

Selena Shipton was the local morning weather girl, but she was damaged goods. She looked like 98% of the featured talent of Girls Gone Wild. She looked like one of those girls, because she was one. She went from being a crazy college Coed with nice tits to being "the reason to get up in the morning." She sucked her way to the local news team, but she would just as soon swallow a bottle of pills, than swallow another load of the news manager's salty man chowder. I knew her story because she and I had a one-night-stand history, and the more she drank, the more she talked. She was a squirter.

I wanted Selena to come over and talk to me, but she ignored me. I doubt she even remembered who I was. She was far more interested in her cell phone. She spent a few minutes texting someone while she polished off a perfect martini, then she disappeared, leaving me to deal with the annoying drunk next to me.

The car dealer had turned his attention to a cute waitress by the bathrooms., leaving the crazy lady to start an unwelcome conversation with me.

"I'm Tanya."

I lit a cigarette. "That's nice."

"I like you. You're artsy. I can tell," she slurred. "You just look artsy. What do you do?"

I didn't want to encourage the conversation to continue. I wanted her to fall off of her bar stool and bust her ass, or knock herself unconscious. I just wanted her to fuck off.

"I'm a writer. I write books," I mumbled.

"What?"

"I said, I write books. Keep your voice down, or you'll get us both kicked out of here."

I knew I was lying, but it felt good. The lying didn't feel great, but it was cool to say I was something, other than a drunk asshole. It felt right to call myself a writer. I knew I hadn't even written so much as a letter since I was in college, but I felt like my little white lie was the start of something great. It filled me with self-worth, which I quickly drank away.

"See, I'm smart! I can tell! You looked like an artsy-fartsy type," she gargled, as she slithered off of her stool, and closer to me. "I only live a couple blocks from here."

"That's really swell, but I don't know why you're telling me. You need to tell a cab driver."

"I don't need a cab! I can FUCKING walk!" She yelled loud enough to get everyone's attention.

I turned away from her and tried to pretend she wasn't there. I tried to get back to my thoughts and enjoy my wine. The last thing I wanted was a drunk, annoying bitch going on about artsy-fartsy bullshit. I wasn't artsy. It wasn't that I couldn't be a writer or an artsy-fartsy type, but at that moment I was just a liar and a drunk.

"You can walk me home. I'm not too drunk to walk," she growled in the loudest whisper I had ever heard. She whispered directly into my ear, "I'm not too drunk to fuck, ya know?"

I turned my head slightly, to acknowledge I heard what she had said.

"What the fuck did you just say to me?'

"Walk me home, and I'm going to suck your cock and let you fuck me any way you want it."

All subtlety was gone, and I had heard enough of her mouth. I could feel the eyes of everyone in the bar burning into me. Tanya was grabbing at my dick, through my jeans, and I was starting feel the wine when the bartender brought me another glass. I didn't remember ordering it, but I chugged the one in my hand, and I stamped out my cigarette, took the next glass in one drink and started fishing in my pockets for money.

I pulled out a wad of wrinkled bills and threw them on the counter. It looked right. I knew I had $19, I had planned to be spending on groceries, and I had drunk about that much in wine. I grabbed Tanya, and dragged the drunk dame out of the bar, by her wrist.

I wasn't too good to turn down a lady making such uninhibited offers. I tried to mask my decision as doing the woman a favor. A woman has needs, and if I was really going to be a writer, I needed things to write about. I thought that there wasn't anything wrong with one more ride on the fucked up Ferris Wheel, but I didn't realize how low I was really sinking.

Tanya reminded me of Angie Cox. She was a sloppy, skinny shell of a beautiful woman, like Ms. Cox. It was oddly comforting how much Tanya had in common with the Pine Drive Prostitute. The awkward, familiar nature of it all sucked me in. It was something about the way she kissed me. There was a desperation there.

We made it back to Tanya's apartment, after several wrong turns, and a quick attempt at a blow job in the alley. Her apartment was on the first floor of a house that looked like it had been condemned. I wasn't sure she wasn't just squatting, because her place was a mess of broken bottles, busted lawn furniture, and moldy garbage.

I didn't get a tour. The only part of her apartment she showed me was the dirty mattress on the floor of her living room. I noticed a few broken light bulbs and a dozen full ashtrays, but I didn't get to look around too much before she started ripping at my jeans and chewing on my cock. It wasn't really enjoyable, but the way she used her hands to tug on me felt amazing. She jerked me off until I got off all over her. Then she got even more rough, and pulled at my dick until I was hard again. After that, it was all a blur of drinking, fucking, drinking, and more fucking.

I hated vodka but since it was the only thing she had at her house, I drank my share and part of hers. Being in her nasty apartment made me question how dirty her lady parts were. I didn't go down on her to find out. She didn't ask me to, anyway, and I kept drinking until I didn't think about it anymore. I was usually sure to be condom-clad before I dove in, but the more I drank, the more unsure I was about being careful.

The next morning, I woke up completely naked, with a cigarette filter still between my fingers, and my dick sticking straight up. I was covered in ashes, and I had to piss like a son of a bitch. Tanya was still passed out, in a prone position, next to me on the dirty mattress. She had her hands tucked under her, holding onto her tits, drooling all over herself, with her ass in the air. I thought about slipping my morning wood in for another wild romp, but in the light she looked like a bigger train wreck than I would usually sink to, and her leathery, bird-like features had a negative result on my erection. She had looked a whole lot better after a bottle of Shiraz.

I thought that she must have put something in my wine, but I remembered everything. I had come there willingly, like the desperate, horny drunk I was, with no self worth. I remembered how it all went down, and how I had forsaken my better judgment to be in a crack house with an ugly woman that may very well have been a diseased whore.

The bathroom was the biggest disaster of all. The bathtub was completely missing, leaving a big yellow ring of dust and filth where it had once been. The mirror above the sink had been smashed, and the sink itself looked like it was stained with blood, diarrhea, and vomit. The toilet didn't look much better, but when I lifted the lid, I was assaulted by a swarm of flies, and a wafting of vile smelling shit. Someone had taken a major dump and just left in the bowl, without any water in it.

Noticing how gross some bathrooms could be was a hazard of the job. There was no saving Tanya's shit hole. It was the nastiest bathroom I had ever seen.

I jiggled the handle on the toilet a couple times, but it didn't flush. I tried the sink, to splash some water on my face, but the water was turned off in her house. With no other choice, I assumed the Superman pose and pissed in the direction of the toilet. When the harsh morning urine hit the shit, it raised a stink that would have gagged a maggot. I coughed and struggled to choke the vomit back.

It might have been less disgusting to have just pissed on the floor.

Unable to wash my hands, I shook myself off and trudged back through the trash to find my clothes. I couldn't get out of there fast enough. I felt like I was supposed to leave money on the night stand or wedged between her ass cheeks, but I had spent all of my cash at the bar. I threw on my shoes and pants and got the fuck out of there before she woke up.

I wasn't proud of myself. I was ashamed that I was so desperate and pathetic, but I knew then that old habits die hard. The drinking felt like a familiar friend. That friend made sure that I became the guy who only called himself a writer, and before my plan was even off the ground, I fell back into making bad choices.

28

After the situation with Holly got weird, I had to stop going to the Coyote Club. I was forced to start doing more of my drinking at home, but buying my wine at the store is how I ran into Dee. We were both shopping at the Save-A- Dime. I had never seen her outside of the club. She had her clothes on, and she looked a lot different. I almost didn't even recognize her.

"Hello, lady."

"I haven't seen you at the club."

"Yeah. I don't think I'm going to be going back there."

"I heard about the thing with you and Destiny."

"Can you please, please, not call her that."

"It's cool. I don't know her real name, but that bitch is a mess."

I hung my head."You heard about that, huh? What did you hear?"

"I'm not sure that's appropriate conversation for the grocery check-out line, you know what I'm sayin'?"

"You might have a point."

"We could go back to my house. I've got some killer bud and a bottle of gin. I was just going to catch up on Real Housewives & Bad Girls Club, but hanging out with you sounds more fun. I promise I won't bite."

"I hope hanging out with me would be more fun that watching reality television. Let's do it!"

Dee lived in a really nice house. It wasn't a very far walk, but she had driven to the Save-A-Dime, so I caught a ride with her. I was surprised at how nice her jeep and her house were. I didn't have any preconceived ideas of how she lived, but it seemed like she was doing very well at the Coyote Club.

The house wasn't a mansion or anything like that, but it was a really nice, newly remodeled, two story French Style, four bedroom house, complete with a pool, hot tub, fireplace, and a bar. It looked like something from Better Homes and Gardens.

Her house made me wish I could get a job shaking my money maker. It also made me curious to know if she had anything else going on the side. I didn't know how to ask, but I was interested in anything that would help me leave my shit-scrubbing job.

I decided to make a joke, and lead into a conversation about how she lived so well. "You have a really nice place. I'm glad to see my tips are going to good use."

Dee was at her bar mixing drinks. "Fuck that! I had to do more than take my clothes off to get this place."

"This sounds like a good story, please continue. I want to know how to have a place like this."

"I don't think you want to do it the same way I did. I got married right after college. I married my speech professor. I gained weight, and my fucking husband decided he wasn't attracted to me anymore."

"He sounds like a real nice guy."

"He's a fucking fascist asshole. That's why he's my

ex-husband. He started screwing around with another one of his students, and I found yoga. He got served with divorce papers, and I got my body back, a really nice house, and his Jeep.

"That is some story. At least it has a happy ending."

"I don't know how happy it is. I took that bastard for everything and I even got the 'twins'."

"The twins? Oh, you have kids? I didn't-"

"No, I was talking about these girls," She laughed, rubbing her tits. "Yep, the best money can buy."

"They are very nice, but I wouldn't have guessed they were fake. I couldn't even see the incision scars."

"That's the point, silly," Dee said, bringing me my drink.

"What's on the agenda, pretty lady?"

"I was thinking we could just chillax. We could have a few gin and tonics, and maybe smoke some of this sweet green I have."

"What the hell is it with everyone? You people do know that marijuana is illegal, right?"

"Oh, I know. I just don't give a shit. I didn't know you were a narcotics agent now. Damn the man!"

"No! I'm cool with what the cool kids are doing. I like to smoke the pot. It just seems like everyone and their sister smokes pot. I didn't realize it was still so popular," I laughed. "Obviously, the war on drugs is very effective."

"It's all good. I like to drink my gin and smoke some chronic. Snoop Dogg was right. It's a real mellow buzz."

"I don't know about Snoop Doggy Dogg, but I'll try anything once, twice if it doesn't kill me."

A little bit of the chronic Dee had mixed with the gin went a long way. I was completely relaxed. I became cool with anything and everything. I sank into the couch more relaxed by the hour, and soon Dee and I were nestled into a messy little pile. Being so close put our hands and faces in some very interesting positions. The interesting positions led to touching and rubbing one another. The rubbing and the touching set up a serious erection that was too hard to hide, and of course I didn't try to hide it, either.

One thing led to another, then to another and another, until Dee and I were going at it like two stoned high school kids who invented the 69.

Things were sloppy and I couldn't really feel anything, until we started having sex. It wasn't anything great. The gin and the chronic had numbed my senses, including my favorite ones. I wasn't even close to getting off when I noticed that I hadn't put a condom on.

I was usually very strict about putting on a glove before I made love, or whatever, no matter how drunk I was. Having unprotected sex was dumb for a lot of reasons. I wasn't trying to catch the crud or anything, and I wasn't going finish inside her without a condom, so I pulled out and considered it a done deal.

She wasn't alright with that idea. "Do you have any condoms?"

"No. I was running to the store. I didn't plan to have sex at the grocery store. We'll have to finish this another time, I guess."

"Don't be silly. You're just gonna have to fuck me in the ass, but be careful!"

"Are you serious?"

She was very serious.

Anal sex wasn't my thing. The idea of sticking my dick in someone's shit shute just didn't sound appealing to me. Dara had tried to get me to try it, but she had never tried to persuade me with gin and chronic.

After we did the deed, I was going to go home, but I was too tired. Dee told me that I didn't have to leave. She offered to let me share her bed. It seemed weird, since there weren't any real feelings between us. It was just ass sex. I didn't protest long.

I insisted on going home for about a minute before I fell asleep.

That night-

I had a dream that I died. In the dream I just fell asleep and didn't wake up. It was the weirdest thing. Destiny, Gilda, Alice, Dara, Dee, Holly, and Monk were all at my funeral. I'm not sure why Monk was there. Other than him, it was a big mess of ladies I had feelings for, or at least had messed around with. The craziest part was seeing them all in the same place at the same time.

Most of the girls were mad at me. They weren't upset because I died. They weren't pissed at me for leaving them. They were angry at me for being an asshole when I was alive.

It wasn't hard to imagine why any of them would be pissed at me. The hardest part of the whole dream was dealing with the idea of falling asleep and not waking up. It made it impossible to fall back asleep. I would have just left. I wanted to be at home, but when I looked over at Dee, it was nice to see a familiar face that wanted me to be there.

She looked scary with her mouth wide open while she was sleeping, but I thought about her inviting me to stay. I threw my arm over her and tried to think about my next move. I thought about what my life would be like if I just stayed with Dee. I couldn't imagine it, but I was getting really tired of feeling like shit and drinking alone.

I never went back to the Coyote Club, but I started seeing her more and more. We had moved from acquaintances at the club to friends with benefits to regular fuck-buddies pretty fast. We never did couple-type things. We just fucked. I'd show up at her house, after her shift at the club. We talked for a little bit, while we caught a buzz. She mostly bitched about the guys at the club. I didn't like hearing about them, but I stuck it out. After she vented, we'd move to the bed room for mediocre sex, before we went to sleep. It was alright, but it never felt completely right.

Then one day the other stripper shoe dropped, and the sexy time stopped too.

I woke up to the sound of a shitty club song started blaring from Dee's phone. It was awful, and the noise pierced my brain. I had the worst hangover of my life. I tried to move, but my whole body hurt, and my head felt like someone had nailed it to the bed, with a huge nail, right through the middle of my forehead. The song was annoying, and Dee wasn't in any hurry to answer the phone, but when she finally did, her voice was even more frustrating. Her usual sweet Alabama drawl was replaced with a nasal butchering of the English language. I would have covered my head with a pillow but it hurt to even breathe.

"Yeah, I'll be there as soon as I can," she spoke into the phone.

She hung up her phone and got up to find clothes. I tried to keep her in bed, but she threw me off. She seemed frustrated.

"Who was that?"

Dee didn't answer. She just kept getting dressed while I watched. At first, I assumed that she didn't hear me. I playfully adjusted myself and smiled at her and offered the same question in a more serious tone.

"Who was that?"

"What the fuck? It's my boss from the club," she snapped. "He needs me to come on and cover for Tori."

Disappointment washed over me. "But I was thinking we might actually do something together today, besides fuck and sleep?"

"I have to get dressed for work."

"Get dressed? You're a stripper," I chuckled. "Isn't that kind of counterproductive?"

"I don't have time for your shit. I have to get ready."

Dee disappeared into the bathroom for a while and came out looking amazing. She looked stripper good. She looked like a picture of sexy when she was going to dance, but for some reason she looked extra hot when she came out of the bathroom.

"Maybe I'll come by and see ya at work. You know I like ya naked, and it might be sexy to watch you shake your money maker."

"You know I can't date customers," Dee finished gathering her things.

"Fuck that. Besides, who said anything about dating. We don't have to put a label on this thing."

"Very funny. Are you gonna get up?"

"I guess. I wanted to get a little more sleep though. Are you kicking me out?

"I just told you, I have to go to work. I just thought you'd leave when I did."

"What? You don't trust me in your house?"

"I don't know. I just don't like having people in my house when I'm not home."

"People? I was just in your vagina, and you don't trust me in your house?"

"Well, it's not like I let you just go poking around unprotected, asshole," she yelled.

"Don't worry. I'll wear a condom until you get home!"

"Shit, I have to go. I don't have time to argue. Lock the door when you leave."

"Have a good day at work, dear! Give lots of lap-dances!"

Dee grabbed her duffel bag and bolted out the door. "Blow me!"

I had a feeling that I had worn out my welcome. Not being there when she came home sounded like the plan of the century. I could have settled for her. We could have lived, miserably-ever-after, but never speaking to Dee again sounded like an even better idea.

Spending a few months at Dee's house made me miss my shitty apartment. I even missed my crazy neighbors. It wasn't the life for everyone. It really wasn't much at all, but it was close to my job and it was home.

It seemed only natural to me that the night that I accepted my apartment as home, was the same night that I came home to find it engulfed in flames.

My apartment, and the entire house it was a part of, became nothing more than a towering inferno. All I could do was watch all of my wine, records, and other worldly possessions go up in flames. In less than a year I my car had been trashed, my mom died, and had to watch as my apartment along with everything I owned burned. It seemed like I had pissed off the wrong God. It was easy to blame God. There was no way to blame my mother's death on anyone. She died of an aneurism in her brain, but the house and the car seemed like the dirty work of someone who had a problem with me.

I wasn't sure, but it seemed like someone was out to get me.

29

Someone had poured gasoline all over my front door. They let it pool under the door, and soak into the carpet on the other side. They emptied the can by pouring a trail leading out of the house, and dumping the rest on the welcome mat on the front porch. Then, they set it on fire and WHOOSH!

Instant wienie roast.

Old houses burn fast, and it didn't take long before the whole house was in flames. The flaming door caught the fuel-saturated carpet on fire. Soon, everything that would burn caught fire. The whole house went up in flames in less time than it took to set the fire. Nobody noticed because nobody cared. When someone finally did notice, they posted about it online, assuming that someone else had already called the fire department. But nobody had called the fire department, at least not until the whole house was a flaming disaster.

When I got home, there were already police and fire fighters on the scene. They were all running around, pointing, yelling, and drenching the remains of the house with their hoses. There wasn't anything left of the house except the smoldering skeleton I once called home.

Someone knew what they were doing when they set the fire, and they didn't care if I was passed out at home, or if I burned alive.

Holly came running as soon as she saw me. I could tell that she had been crying. "HARLOW!"

I must have been standing there for a while before she noticed me. I don't think I moved. I just watched the fireman douse the smoldering flames.

"I'm so glad you're alright. We didn't know if you were in there or not," She said. "Monk couldn't get out. I left him in his cage. He didn't survive…"

She started crying again. I already knew the story before she told me. I knew as soon as I saw the make-up running down her face. It was also obvious because she wasn't holding the little fucker.

I was pleasantly surprised at how happy I was to see Holly alive, but I wasn't concerned about her dog. She told me that Dan had moved out the week before. I didn't care about him either.

Knowing that all I had left were the clothes on my back, and the money I had in the bank, was a pretty shitty feeling. I knew Holly had lost everything, too. I just didn't care. I didn't care about Dan, Holly, or her stupid little dog, and I didn't care to stand around and watch the firefighters extinguish what was left of the house.

I only had four-hundred dollars of my next month's rent, but I wasn't going to have to pay it. I would have to use the money to find a place to stay, and something to drink. I decided to get the drink first. When I got to the liquor store, I didn't pay any attention to what kind of booze I bought, or how much it cost. I just grabbed the first bottle of wine that caught my eye and left the store.

After I got checked into my shitty little motel room,

I realized that I had bought a two hundred dollar 2010 Sassicaia.

I didn't take my time enjoying the wine's subtle notes, or what kind of finish it had. I took the bottle in one hand, and what was left of my dignity in the other, and went for a walk. If I was homeless, I was going to drink my high-dollar wine like a Sterno bum.

I hated staying in motels, but, at the moment, I didn't have any other option.

The bottle was almost empty when I noticed that a beat-up blue van had been behind me for a while. I noticed the van when I left the motel, and again when I left the liquor store. I didn't think anything about it, but I had been walking for a while, and it must have been following me the whole time. It might have even been following me from the time I left my blazing apartment.

After a few more blocks, I stopped and turned around. I look directly at the old van and the driver knew I had spotted them. I was surprised that he didn't try anything crazy. The van just sped past me and turned off a few blocks down the street, so I couldn't see who was driving. I didn't even think to look at the license plates.

It was clear that someone was fucking with me, but I wasn't interested in their bullshit. I was too numb for that.

I was upset about losing my records, and everything else I owned. I was also upset because I knew I was going to be staying in a crappy motel for a while. I had pissed Dee off, and fucked that up too soon. In the future I planned to make sure my house wasn't going down in flames before I burned anymore bridges.

30

When Alice called me, I was really surprised. I had been hiding in my motel for days, and I hadn't seen or heard from her since Destiny's wedding. I had never called her, and I figured that she had forgotten about me. I had been so wrapped up in my own chaos that I had almost forgotten about her, and that incredible kiss she planted on me.

Gilda had taken my mind off of Alice and Destiny for a while. After that, all of my swirling chaos had taken over. I was excited to hear from her, but I wasn't sure I wanted her to see me living out of a ratty hotel when she suggested we get together.

Alice said that she was only going to be in town for a little while. She was looking for someone to hang out with, and I was her first choice. She had been visiting her parents, but they were pretty boring.

"You didn't call."

"I'm sorry. I've been trying to sort my shit out and get on track. It's a full time job."

"That's good," she said. "I've been thinking about

you."

I lied (to make myself look good). "I've been thinking about that kiss."

"I've thought about that a time or two myself."

I wasn't one for long phone conversations, so we agreed to meet for drinks. I didn't want to take her to any of my usual haunts, so we agreed to meet at a place I'd never been, one that was within walking distance of my motel. I was nervously excited to see Alice, but I wasn't sure how I felt about going to a bar called Scooters.

It sounded like a gay bar, but Scooters was a sports bar. It was full of televisions. I saw Alice sitting at the bar. She waved at me. I made my way toward her through the sports fans.

Scooters didn't serve wine, and it was hard to hear each other talking. More strikes against them.

Alice smiled when she yelled, "Why didn't you call me?"

"I assumed you were busy," I yelled back. "I was pretty sure you didn't have time for my shit."

"I told you I liked you, Harlow. I gave you my number."

"I took from our conversation that you liked my potential. I still don't think I have myself together enough to be the guy you say you were looking for.

"I may have been a little harsh on you. You were a mess at the wedding, but I wanted to apologize."

"For what?"

"I didn't have the right to lecture you like that. You're a great guy. I can't even imagine how it must have felt to deal with the whole Destiny thing all those years, and then have to watch her get married. I was being insensitive. I think I was even a little jealous."

"I'm not mad. You made a lot of sense. I was a wreck, and I disrespected you. The Destiny thing was hard. I had the biggest thing for her for the longest time, but it doesn't matter anymore."

"You're not going to try to steal her away from Elmer?"

"Not a chance. I let my stupid little crush on her dictate entirely too much of my life. I blew a lot of other opportunities, and never even asked other girls I liked out because they were friends with Destiny."

"This sounds interesting. Tell me more."

"Do you remember me mentioning that story of the girl I knew, that I thought was too cool to approach?"

"I remember you saying something about that, before the infamous kiss."

"You were that girl. Destiny was the girl that had my attention, but that was because I always thought that you were too cool to give me the time of day."

"You never asked."

"You were too awesome, and I thought you only dated college guys. I had hope that maybe Destiny would fall for me, and I could be happy with her, but you were the girl that I was too nervous to even talk to. You're beautiful. Back then you were the coolest. You were a year or so older, had a cool car, the best records, and great taste in music. I had you upon this unobtainable pedestal, higher than Destiny. I'm not sure, but I think that's a pretty big compliment."

"Harlow, we hung out all the time. You should have said something that might have made it worth your time. I'm only a year or two older than you, and I never thought about that. You were pretty cool back then, too. You have great taste, and you were always the nicest of all of the guys we hung out with. You drank a little too much, but a good woman might have been able to distract you from that. A good woman might have appreciated you, and been better for you than you obsessing on Destiny for years."

"Are you saying that I might have stood a chance?

You noticed me?"

"We're friends, Harlow. We've been friends for as long as I can remember. I didn't sit around thinking about you at night all the time, but sure, I thought about you. I don't care what anyone thinks. A man and a woman cannot be 'friends' without thinking about what it would be like to see each other naked, what it would be like, and things like that."

"Why didn't you say anything?"

"I thought about it, but it was obvious to everyone that you had a big hard-on for Destiny. Nobody wanted to get in the middle of an obsession like that. She's a cool chick. You're a cool guy, but I didn't want to compete with Destiny or your obsession. I didn't have to. I had my own things, hey, but now, however, here we are." She smiled and touched my leg.

"I spent a lot of time trying to make myself the bad boy I thought Destiny wanted, and never thought about what I wanted."

"Damn. That's hot!"

"What? I don't understand how my pathetic attempted to win over a woman I never told about my feelings, is hot. What do you mean?"

"You followed her, and tried to be the man she wanted without even telling her how you felt. That's romantic. You should have told her. She might have fallen for it."

"It wasn't completely selfless. I enjoyed the wild nights of drinking and other bullshit, but while I was getting into being a bad boy asshole, she was getting over the bad boy types."

"You know what kind of girls like bad boys, don't you?"

"I'm not sure. Is there a certain type?"

"They're always the immature little bitches who don't know what they want, or the girls who want to play mommy. They want a bad boy they can fix and take care of, and that's fucked-up."

"I'm not sure your assessment is one hundred percent accurate, but it makes sense."

"It's not my assessment. It's something I read in my Women's Studies class."

"You took Women's studies? I thought that was only for crunchy, man-hating lesbians, and crazy protest-sign-wielding feminists."

"For the record, being a feminist doesn't automatically mean I'm a lesbian, or that I even kiss my girlfriends on the weekends. I hate that shit. It also doesn't mean that I don't shave or that I hate men, either."

"I didn't mean to strike a nerve. I was only joking."

"Make jokes, but feminism is about equality. It's pro-women, not anti-men. I'm not saying that's always the case, but that's how I see it. That's how I was taught. I'm a supporter of equal rights for men and women. I believe in strong women, and I don't think any woman needs a man or anyone else to tell her what to do with her body."

"That makes perfect sense. Sign me up. I agree with all of that. I love women."

"You love getting drunk and fucking women. I could probably get my feminist card taken away for even hanging out with you."

"You actually get a little card? Is it pink?"

"No, smart-ass. We don't have little cards."

"I guess I was wrong about feminists all these years. I didn't spend a lot of time thinking about them, but my perception was way off."

"Let that be a lesson to you. Don't be so damn judgmental. Not every clown is a serial killer. Not every cop likes donuts, and not every feminist is a crazy man-hating lesbian. Most of the ones I know aren't. I'm not. I like guys."

"Are there any guys that you might be into at the moment?"

"I don't know, there might be one or two. One of them is kind of a mess though. He might be more trouble than he's worth."

"He might be, but it might be worth it. He might not be your type, though."

"There you go, being judgmental again. I'll have you know, I was a virgin until college, but once I got out to UCLA, I was one of those girls with a tight pussy and loose morals."

"I had no idea. I'm sorry if it seems like I'm not paying attention. I just need a moment to play with all of that in my head..."

"I even lost my V card to a much older man. He was my philosophy professor."

"And, - I'm hard."

"You're reprehensible."

"You're gorgeous."

"You're drunk."

"You're still gorgeous."

"You're only saying that because you're drunk. You don't mean it."

"Yes, I do. I'm always drunk, but I still mean it. I've thought it for a very long time."

"We've both been drinking. Maybe we should just call it a night.'

"Maybe."

She kept smiling at me over the table. She had a champagne smile. It made it impossible not to smile back at her.

Without much more conversation, we agreed to go back to my motel room, as long as she let me pick up before she came in. I warned her that it wasn't much of a place. She promised not to hold it against me.

When we got back to the motel, she looked into my eyes like she was looking for something, but before either of us could say another word, our faces collided with a kiss. She looked into my eyes for almost another solid minute. It was like she was making sure I knew what I was getting myself into. It might have been that she was looking for sincerity. The sincerity was there, and it was followed with a lot more kissing. I never had time to clean up the room.

I was sure Alice was going to come to her senses and run for the door at any moment, but she didn't. She walked me over to the bed, with a bashful hesitation I hadn't seen in her before. She seemed genuinely nervous and excited about being with me.

We kissed a little more, but Alice pulled away and looked at me one more time. "I hope you know I'm not one of your bridesmaids, or any other little bimbo."

"I know that."

"I'm not Destiny either."

"I know that too, I know."

31

I knew hooking up with Alice was the real deal. I knew
that there was no turning back. There would never be
another drunken mistake, one night stand, or bad
decision with a woman's name. I also never had to worry
about waking up next to another woman, and worry
about remembering her name, like I did with...what's her
name?

I had spent a long time on a vacation in Drunksville,
taken with any woman who wanted to spend time with
me, but shit got into perspective real fast when I woke
up next to an unknown girl from a bar.

I don't know what woke me up. I didn't know
where the hell I was, when I woke up. I must have had
way too much to drink, because it took a long time to
realize that I was in my apartment, and there was a
naked girl in my bed with me. I couldn't remember
where I had met her.

I had to take a minute while she was still passed out
to collect myself.

My vision was just about as fuzzy as my memory.

Mixing beer and wine had that effect on me. I couldn't remember where I had been drinking, or where I had found the girl, but from what I could see, I could have found her anywhere but a beauty pageant.

Since I was awake, I got up and headed to the bathroom. According to the girl's watch, it was already after noon, and my bladder felt like it was holding an entire barrel of wine. Judging from my dragon breath, I must have been drinking whiskey, too. I would have also been willing to bet that it was some cheap shit, too.

By the time I was done pissing, my head was pounding. I knew I had drunk more than my share of wine, beer and whiskey. It was unlike me to mix my alcoholic drinks like that. I usually stuck with what I started drinking at the beginning of the night. I was going to feel less than myself the next day, no matter what, but mixing alcohol was a good way to feel like complete shit. I liked drinking, but I wasn't a total fucking idiot. I reached for my toothbrush.

I heard the troglodyte stirring in the bedroom. "Harlow?"

She was awake, and she knew my name.

I poked my head out of the bathroom, as I brushed the vileness out of my mouth. My vision had cleared, and I was surprised to see that girl in my bed wasn't a mutant after all. She was cute.

As she stood up, she wrapped herself in my bed sheet. She looked to be about 5'6 or 5'7. She was a petite blonde with a sweet face. Watching her wrap her perky tits in the sheet made it nearly impossible to make eye contact, but she had an enchanting pair of peepers too. They were an innocent, baby blue.

"I thought you'd left," she said, with an embarrassed smile.

"No, I live here. Why in the hell would I leave a strange girl in my house?" I replied, with my toothbrush still in my mouth.

"Strange, huh?"

"I didn't mean it like that." I said, after spitting into the sink.

"So, you mean 'strange' in a good way?"

I rinsed out my tooth brush and grabbed a shirt, which smelled kind of clean, from the bathroom floor. I couldn't even remember this girl's name, and she was already pissing me off. It was time for her to go.

"Look-"

"You don't even know my name do you?"

"Of course I do!" I said, racking my brain for the answer.

She had me. I didn't have a clue. I just wanted a cigarette, and her out of my apartment.

"So, what is it?"

I rummaged around through some papers on the counter looking for a smoke to kill time. If I delayed long enough, her name was sure to come back to me. I hoped.

"Have you seen my cigarettes?"

"Maybe. What's my name, Harlow?"

It was on the tip of my brain, but I really, really wanted that damn cigarette. My head was beginning to pound with an annoying rhythm, making this pretty little thing's voice feel like thumbtacks in my forehead.

"Just tell me where my damn smokes are, and then I'll play your stupid game," I growled.

The girl just rolled her eyes. "You ran out of cigarettes last night."

"Really?"

"Yep, now, do you remember my name or not?"

"I give up. I'm a jerk! I can't remember your name!"

"I can't believe this, after everything you said last night. You don't even know my name? You really are one sorry son of -"

"Hey, I already said I was a jerk. I'm really sorry. What do you want me to do?"

"I guess since you can't remember, it doesn't matter, huh?"

"I wish I could remember, because, before you started bustin' my balls, I thought you were pretty good looking."

"What about last night? Do you remember last night?"

I could see our clothes were all over the floor, leading from the front door to the bedroom. I was drawing another blank. "Nothing."

The girl's mouth fell open. "Unbelievable!"

I was starting to remember meeting this girl at The Pour House, but I must have drunk a hell of a lot to forget her name.

In a huff, the girl began to gather her clothes, as I checked the refrigerator for a drink. The fridge was empty, but, to my surprise, there was a half empty bottle of whiskey on the floor. I grabbed the bottle and took two big swigs. It was warm, but it burnt good going down.

I was already feeling better, but the nameless chick was still pissed, and already dressed. I had missed the reverse strip show.

Her hand was on the door knob. "Last chance, loser. What's my name?"

"Sara, Kelly, Megan, - throw me a bone here. Hell, I don't know!"

"You don't know because I never told you," she laughed. "And the reason you don't remember last night is because we passed out before we got to third base. Next time, let's skip the foreplay."

"Next time?"

She walked out without saying another word. She

was a cruel mistress. She seemed so playful while she had my balls in a vice. She knew I didn't know her name, and she tortured me anyway. She was a cutie, but something told me that she had a strange sexy side. That intrigued me, and made me like the threat of a 'next time'.

I stood there speechless, with thoughts of her naked dancing in my head, when she popped her head back in the door. "By the way, my name is Paige. See you tonight, tiger."

I did see Paige again. I saw her several times. I saw a lot of her and her sweet little body. We never gave a serious run at a relationship. We just got drunk together, and messed around on a very regular basis, until she fell for the lead singer of The Broderick.

She left to follow the band on tour, and I had another drink.

32

I lost my job as a janitor because of missing too many days. Alice worked as a nurse for Planned Parenthood, but I wasn't really concerned about not having a job. My mom had left me some money, and I got a few thousand more from her life insurance. For all of the shit that she gave me, she actually cared enough to leave a healthy chunk of change. I assumed she'd leave whatever she had to Garrett and Rick, but I didn't know her as well as I thought.

Alice encouraged me to use the money and the time off to move to Indianapolis, get a car, and work on my writing. A new city and a steady gal pal made me feel like I was getting a new lease on life. I was able to get a fresh start and keep my nose clean. I finally had a nice place, and Alice stayed with me on a regular basis. We didn't officially live together. She already had her own place a few blocks away, but she spent a whole hell of a lot more time at my apartment than at home. She said that she liked my apartment better.

Eventually, more and more of her stuff ended up at my apartment. She bought groceries and wine, and even did some cleaning. It felt nice, and we started talking about her letting her apartment go and living in sin, until she could make an honest man out of me.

Things got pretty serious, pretty fast between Alice and me.

We even talked about buying a house together, and making it a home, then taking things to the next step. The next step included talk of marriage and having kids. I didn't really enjoy those kinds of conversations as much. I knew Alice wanted all of those things, and she was the only woman that had ever made me consider changing my mind about wanting them. I'd sworn I'd never get married. I knew I wasn't the sort of guy who needed to have a child, but when Alice and I got together, all of that changed. I loved her so much, I was thinking about how cool our wedding would be, and how awesome spending the rest of my life with her would be. I even knew that any kid we created would be the coolest kid on the planet, but when it was time to start moving on those plans I froze.

Alice made a few comments about what kind of engagement ring she wanted. We didn't talk about it much. It came up, but she knew it scared the shit out of me. Settling down, with my busted history of screwing things up, meant I had the chance to fuck this up, too. I wanted the simple life with a beautiful woman, but I was terrified of it, too.

I was able to tuck away my bullshit, though, and I started looking at engagement rings.

The cost of something worthy of being worn by my lovely lady was a lot of money. I was weird about spending the money. I had zero problems with spending hundreds of dollars on records or wine, but buying an engagement ring for a woman I loved felt like taking a bullet to the head, not that I actually knew how a bullet to the head felt. It was clear that what was tripping me up the most was how serious of a commitment it was.

I was scared of hurting Alice. I didn't have much faith in marriage. I had never seen anyone make a marriage work successfully. It felt like I was jumping head first into something that was doomed from the start.

Even when I found the perfect ring, I couldn't bring myself to slap down my secret stash of cash on it. I didn't know why, but something felt wrong. I kept an eye on the ring, and almost bought it twice. I wanted to get it, but I froze every time. It just felt too heavy to follow through on.

Alice didn't force the issue. She seemed confident that everything would happen when it was time. I wasn't sure. I tried to tell myself that Alice and I would be the exception to the rule. We would be the ones to make a marriage work. I also told myself I was going to be a successful writer. I lied to myself a lot. I wanted both of the things I told myself to be true, but I couldn't convince myself, and the engagement ring stress affected my writing.

Still, I was writing more than I had in years. I just wasn't sure I had been producing anything of any substance. I had been writing a lot, and sending stories and articles to every magazine, website, and lit journal that would take submissions. I didn't really feel like I knew what I was doing. I was just writing.

The other chaos was gone, though, because I did my drinking at home, and I used the time while Alice was away at work to get as much writing in as I could, and spent the rest of my time with her. Alice never read any of my stuff. She said she wasn't my target audience, but she kept encouraging me. Her encouragement kept me writing.

I wasn't the only person doing some writing.

I didn't even know people still wrote letters. I thought in a world full of email, texting and Tweeting, a good old-fashioned letter was dead. I was wrong. Letter writing may have been on its deathbed, but I was surprised as hell to get an old-fashioned paper and envelope letter.

The mail came every day around the same time, and since I didn't have a real job, I was the one that plucked it from its rusty metal box. Most of it was the usual pile of bills, ads, and bullshit, and then, one day, there was a letter from Dara.

The letter was a jumbled mess of pleasantries, and an interest in catching up. With the letter was an invitation to her art exhibit, in a Nashville gallery. She still lived in Tennessee, and I was initially not interested in driving three hours for much of anything. Seeing Dara would be the only reason to make the drive. I hadn't even realized how much I wanted to see her, until I got the letter. The letter wasn't anything special, but it really shook me up.

It got me thinking and over-thinking things I was sure of. That stupid letter had me thinking about Dara all the time, especially when I was drinking. I thought about how she would look. I even pondered what things would be like if we tried to date again. We were young and dumb the first time around. Our relationship was mostly a lot of getting fucked-up and having awesome sex. The sex was one of the things I missed about her, but I knew having sex with Dara again meant ending things with Alice. There was no way to rekindle things with Dara, or even just try to hook up with her again, without hurting Alice.

I didn't want to hurt Alice. She was incredible, and we had forged an adult relationship. I felt stupid for even considering throwing it all away for one more ride on the merry-go-round with Dara. I felt like an idiot, but it was a familiar feeling. Old habits die hard, and making bad choices came easy to me.

I remembered the energy I felt when I was around Dara. She was a sexy little crazy train, and I knew there was no way to make a serious relationship work with her, but I was very interested in a few sins of the flesh. Having sex with Dara wasn't a sure thing. She had only expressed interest in catching up and inviting me to her art exhibit. There wasn't anything to read between the lines.

For all I knew, Dara was dating someone. She might have turned gay. She might have only invited me to be nice. She could still have been harboring hurt feelings from my decision to end our relationship, but she might have been thinking the same things I was thinking. She might have invited me, just to see me and try to reignite the spark we had before.

The only thing that was clear to me was that if Dara was able to spin my head so easily, my shit was still fucked-up. I was still the same selfish sonofabitch. I had only been playing house with Alice, and my habit of screwing shit up would eventually lead to me hurting Alice. I felt like the only way to save her the big hurt later was to end it before things got any more serious. I called it preservation through destruction.

It didn't seem completely unhealthy to end things with her, due to my hesitation about buying the damned engagement ring. I knew I needed to end things with Alice before I fucked it up royally. The letter from Dara was my sign. At least I tried to convince myself that it was a sign.

Some people might think everything happens for a reason. I think those people are full of shit. I only believe it when it is to my benefit.

33

I had thought things were over when I threw up in Dara's mouth, but she was pretty cool about the whole thing. She showed up at my house the next morning after the drugs had worn off, and we were both cleaned up. I knew it was her when I heard the knock on my door.

It took all of the courage in the world to open the door, but she was standing there in a long, yellow rain coat, with a smile on her face.

"Aren't you going to invite me in?"

"I don't know. I feel really stupid about the whole vomit thing."

"Let's not talk about it. It happened. It was pretty fucked-up. Let's just move on. It's over. It was gross, and I hope it never happens again, but it's over."

Dara was always coming out of nowhere with weird and random sex facts. "Did you know a pig's orgasm can last up to 30 minutes."

"Lucky pig."

"I don't know. It might start to not feel as good after a while."

"I'm sure I don't know."

"You're saying you've never fucked a pig in your days?"

"I might have boned a few chicks that would pass for pigs but beggars can't be choosers."

"Wow! You can be an asshole!"

We both laughed for at least a solid minute before Dara got the most serious look I had ever seen in her starry eyes. She gave me a smile. It wasn't her usual smile. It was more of a nervous smile.

"You should let me paint you. I like to paint assholes."

"I don't think I'd be a very good subject for a painting. I don't have a good side, but thanks for calling me an asshole, twice, by the way."

"I'm serious. I like to paint assholes."

"I get it. I know I can be a real dick sometimes, but that is a pretty weird reason to want to paint me."

"Harlow, you're not listening. Not dicks, I paint assholes. I want you to model yours for me. It's a series I started before we started dating. I haven't done one since we've been together."

"What the fuck? You mean you paint portraits of people's rectums? You actually paint pictures of actual assholes?"

"Yes, assholes, rectums, brown eye, shit shute, whatever you want to call them. Yes. I like to have people bend over and spread their cheeks, then I paint pictures of their perfectly puckered posteriors with pastels and abstract colors. When I'm finished, they look like fantastic flowers."

I didn't really know how to respond, so I just blurted out the first thing that popped out. "That's pretty fucked-up. I think there is something wrong with you. Do you think this is something a normal person does?"

"Fuck you," Dara snapped. "How dare you fucking

judge me. You get drunk, and stick your dick in anything that will have you, and you have the balls to give me shit over beautiful Georgia O'Keeffe-style paintings of something so many people think is so dirty. You're the fucked-up one."

"I'm sorry," I said. "I think I might have just been projecting. I don't get it, but I was wrong to judge you like that."

There was another awkward silence before she played her ace in the hole. "Now you have to let me paint your asshole."

I looked around the room at the flowers on the wall. I thought about the other paintings of hers I had seen, and I could see a blatant rectum in every one of them.

The next thing I knew, I had dropped my pants, and I was spreading my ass cheeks to let Dara paint a picture of my anus. I tried to get wasted before the thing went down, but it didn't work. I was humbled and immortalized on the canvas with my butt-hole exposed for the whole word to see. It was the single, most uncomfortable moment I had ever experienced without my pants on. That was about the time things got weird between Dara and me.

We still dated for a little while, but it didn't last long. I took exception to her painting asses. I didn't like the idea of other guys dropping their pants for her. It wasn't really a trust issue. The whole thing was just too weird for me.

34

After I got the letter from Dara I could feel myself pushing Alice away. I didn't tell her that I had gotten the invitation and the letter from Dara. I didn't give her the engagement ring, and I started staying out at the bar later and later every night. I didn't stay out to be a dick. I just had a lot on my mind. I was thinking about Dara too much, and seeing Alice made me feel guilty.

My history of making bad choices seemed to give me no choice but to fuck-up everything with Alice for one more wild ride with Dara.

I loved Alice, but the allure of the chaotic chick would always be there. Yet, I knew if anything happened between Dara and me, it might be white hot, but it would only burn out and fade away like it did the last time.

I didn't even know if Dara was interested in me anymore. I wasn't sure I'd still be into her. I played it out a thousand different ways in my head. Most of the thoughts led to me jerking off, while Alice was at work.

Dara felt like cheating on Alice, but it was exciting.

There was a chance that Dara only invited me because the exhibit was going to be her Assholes exhibition, and maybe she thought that I might want to see my winking sphincter hanging in a gallery.

I didn't know how to react when Dara told me that my asshole was going to be hanging in an art gallery. I had never seen the actual painting. I wasn't sure I wanted to, and I wasn't sure I wanted everyone to see my butt-hole on display, but I went anyway

By the time I left for Nashville, Alice and I passed like ships in the night.

I never told her about the showing. I didn't want her to come with me. It would have been too much like the dream I had about my funeral. I knew it was a dick move, but I didn't even tell her that I was going to Nashville. I just left her a note that said that I was going to be gone for a couple days.

I was already in Tennessee by the time she got the note. I had stopped at a truck stop to take a piss, and I was standing in a stall draining the dragon when I got the call. I didn't even need to look at my phone. I knew her ringtone, but as I went to silence my phone I dropped it into the toilet. It dropped into the bowl, and sank into the golden water. The phone went silent, and I thought about leaving it in there, but I knew I was going to have to fish it out.

There wasn't any reason to fuck around. I wasn't going to be able to flush the piss down, without risk of losing the phone completely. I had to plunge my hand in, grab the phone, wrap it in paper towels until I could come up with a better option, and wash my hands.

Not having a phone felt weird, but it also felt liberating.

Since I was in Nashville, I decided that I needed to hit a few of my regular haunts like the coffee shop Jack and I had hung out in, the bar where I first met Dara, and my favorite record store. There were a lot of my old stomping grounds that I wanted to see, but I also decided to look up Gilda.

I hadn't seen her since she had moved back to Nashville. She had come back to Indiana to get her stuff, without stopping by to see me. We hadn't even talked on the phone.

Trying to find Gilda wasn't easy. I checked all of the usual places she liked. I didn't know if she would want to see me if I found her. I didn't know where she lived. I didn't know if she was working anywhere. I was coming up with nothing, until I was checking out at the record store.

The guy behind the counter was someone who knew Jack, Gilda, and me pretty well. At one time, he was good about turning us onto new music and hooking us up with good deals on vinyl. He recognized me and started a conversation.

"You are Gilda's friend, right?"

"Yeah, I think. I haven't seen her for a while. I'm just in town for the night."

"Are you going to her show tonight?"

"Honestly, I didn't know she had a show. Do you have the information on it?"

He handed me a pink flyer. "She's been playing a lot lately, and that club's pretty cool. It should be a good show. You should check it out."

"I will. Thanks a lot."

I handed over the money for the records I was buying, but I didn't take my eyes off of the pink paper. It said that Gilda was playing at a place called The Cat House. I had never heard of it, but I loved to hear Gilda sing and I wanted to see her, even if it was for the last time.

After I paid for my records and got directions to the

The Cat House for later, I headed to the gallery. I wasn't excited to see my ass on display for everyone to see, but I was nervously excited to see Dara. I didn't know how it was going to go down, but even if things didn't reignite, I would have my closure.

Dara had dyed her hair a dirty sea-foam green color I had never seen on her before. She was always changing her hair color, and she looked as attractive and eccentric as ever. She had on a short, little zebra-striped skirt with a fuzzy orange sweater, and a pair of knee-high Doc Martin boots.

She noticed me as soon as I walked in the door. She bolted from the conversation she was in, and jumped into my arms. I nearly fell backwards, but I was able to catch her, and endure the bear hug she attacked me with.

It took me a minute to figure out what was different about Dara. She was still gorgeous, but she had added a nose ring to her beautiful face. It was just a single ring through her left nostril. It wasn't even that noticeable, but it was a turn-off for me. I didn't like facial piercings, and I really didn't like it on Dara. It took away from her multi-color enhanced natural beauty.

Once she was finished squeezing the life out of me, she kissed my cheek and dragged me around the gallery to introduce me to everyone she said was important. I didn't know what to say to any of her people, but it was nice to be pulled around, hand in hand, and to be introduced to everyone. It made me feel pretty special.

It didn't take long to make all of the introductions, and when we had made our rounds, she led me to the refreshments area. She poured me a glass of the Pinot she had stashed under the table.

"Pinot Noir is still your favorite, right?"

"Yes. You have a pretty good memory."

"I made sure to have one on hand in case you showed up. I can't believe you're here. I didn't think you'd really come."

"You sent me an invite. I had to come. Who doesn't want to see a painting of their own butt-hole."

I looked around at all of the paintings hanging in the gallery. None of them looked like asses. They really did look more like flowers. It made me wish I didn't know what I was really looking at, but I still wondered which one was mine.

Dara didn't seem interested in talking about her art. She was more interested filling a paper plate with chocolate chip cookies and talking about the past. She instantly brought up the old days.

After she poured herself a glass of wine and sat me down on a huge, fuzzy, green couch, we continued our trip down memory lane.

"Do you still have the pink Malibu?" I asked.

"Nope, I sold it."

"Really? That surprises me. You loved that car. What are you driving now?"

"I get around," Dara said, before she thrust her plate into my face. "You should really try the cookies. They're great."

"You really have a thing for these cookies."

"Actually, as a child, I was kidnapped by being lured into a car with a cookie. No joke. I wasn't a dumb kid. I just really loved cookies."

"That's pretty weird. Did that really happen?"

"Yes, sir. I don't remember it, but my mom told me that they just took me to Chucky Cheese and dropped me off back at home. They were the best kidnappers ever."

"This sounds like a load of shit."

"I'm serious. The lady down the block wanted a daughter, and she tried to buy me from my mom, and when mom said no, she kidnapped me," Dara declared. "I thought I told you this story."

"That's pretty fucked-up. I think I would have

remembered it."

There was a minute or more where we just sat there and didn't say anything. She acknowledged the people in the gallery there to see her work. I looked around at the assholes all over the wall. I wondered again which one was mine. I hadn't seen the finished piece of ass.

"So, which one of these is mine?"

"You don't know? I figured you'd recognize it."

"I don't have a clue."

Dara burst into laughter. "There is a joke in there somewhere about not being able to find your own ass, but I'll show you where it is."

We walked though a few groups of people, to the back of the room. We had to stop a few times, for people to pay Dara compliments. They were right. Her paintings were fantastic. I couldn't even tell that most of them were someone's butt-hole. If I wasn't privy, to the information, I would have never guessed.

When we finally made it to the back of the gallery, I saw a huge framed canvas splashed with purple and green paint, that formed the image of my fuzzy brown eye. I liked it. It was the biggest painting in the exhibit. I thought that it might have been a statement about how big of an asshole I really was, but I didn't want to ask. I didn't have to.

"The biggest asshole in the room, for the biggest asshole in the room," Dara confirmed.

"I'm flattered, but why did you even invite me? You must really think I'm-"

"I miss you, Harlow."

"I miss you too."

"No, I don't think you get it. I loved you. You were my first serious love."

"We had some really good times."

"I really miss you. When you stopped calling me, and it was obvious you were avoiding me, I was crushed.

I didn't know what to do with myself."

"It's a long story. I know it sounds stupid to say it out loud, but it wasn't you. It was me."

"You couldn't come up with anything less cliche than that bullshit?"

"I'm sorry. I don't know how to explain it. Things just got weird. I freaked out a bit and put some space between us."

"You put a lot of fucking space between us. That's why I sent you the invite to this little soiree. I wanted to see you again, but most of all I wanted you to see what kind of an asshole you are."

"I get it."

Dara was getting louder, and most of the crowd had turned their attention to us.

"NO! You don't fucking get it. If you didn't want me to paint you, I wouldn't have forced it. I just wanted to be with you. I loved you! I still love you!"

"Wow! There it is. I don't know what to-"

"I already know what you're going to say. You're going to say; 'I'm sorry, but I love someone else.' You're going to tell me; 'I'm in a serious relationship and I can't be with you.' I'm surprised you didn't bring your girlfriend with you, or is this not the sort of thing Alice is in to?"

"You are seriously overreacting here. Can we go talk somewhere a little more private?" I began, but it occurred to me that I hadn't told her about being in a relationship. She could have assumed, but I know I didn't tell her Alice's name. "Wait a minute. How did you know about Alice?"

She only froze for a moment. "I'm sure someone told me. I don't know who. It doesn't matter. You're changing the subject!"

"I don't know who would have told you. We don't have a lot of mutual friends. I wish I knew who it was.

I'm not pissed or anything. I was just curious how you knew and how you even got my address."

"This is stupid. I'm sorry I invited you."

"There's no reason to be sorry."

"You can leave. I have other guest I need to attend to."

I should have told her that she was wrong. I wanted to tell her that I wanted to be with her, but I knew I didn't want to be with her in the way she wanted. I knew that any spark that was there between us would flash and fade away fast. It would probably lead to one of us getting burned.

I didn't say anything, and Dara didn't wait for me to say anything. She disappeared into the crowd and I made a hasty retreat. I felt that it was the best thing for everyone. There wasn't any need to drag things out, or cause a scene.

Dara was right. I had Alice, and I was already well on my way to screwing that up. Telling Dara that I still had feelings for her would be the ultimate way to turn things into a complete disaster. It might have been fun, but nothing would ever come of it. I knew that I wasn't able to make things work with anyone.

Like Alice, Dara was able to do better than me. There was someone out there who could give her what she needed more than I could. I wasn't so down on myself that I didn't think these women didn't really love me. I loved them, too, but I wasn't any good for them. I loved them enough to protect them from me and my bullshit.

Sadly, Alice and Dara weren't the only ones I had fallen for. I had already made plans to go see Gilda play at The Cat House. I knew seeing Gilda again was going to bring back old feelings about her, but I was still enough of an emotional masochist to want to see her.

I told myself I was just going to see her face, and

listen to her music. I didn't need to drop myself back into her life. I thought that if I did that, I was sure to fuck up anything good she had going for her. Part of me thought that the third time around might be different. The third time is the charm, they say, but I knew better.

I was better served to just take in a few songs, glance at her beautiful face, say hello, and get back home. There was already enough crap to deal with waiting for me in Indiana. I didn't need to pile on anymore for myself or anyone else. I just needed to see Gilda one last time. I needed the same closure which seeing Dara again gave me.

The Cat House was a pretty cool little music bar. Their logo was a rockabilly cat, like something out of a Brian Setzer wet dream. The name of the place made me think it was a gay bar.

It sounded like a place for lesbians to pick up chicks, but I was wrong.

When I walked in, I could see Gilda talking to a young hipster couple, and a guy who could have easily passed for Kurt Cobains' twin brother. I decided not to interrupt.

I figured I'd just talk to her after the show. I was content ordering a drink, and looking around the place.

The first thing I noticed was the wall of autographed band pictures. The pictures were mostly small-time blues artists, local bands, and a few under-rated big names that had played the Cat House.

I was pleasantly surprised to see that Gilda's dad was one of the recording artists on the wall.

It wasn't a very big place. It was big enough to have a stage and a few tables, but most of the space was taken up by an S-shaped bar, and a dance floor in front of the stage. Most of the place was black and chrome, but there was some red leather on the booths and bar stools. It was a cool set up, and it was lit up with pink neon lights and classy alcohol adds. None of the tacky NASCAR shit I saw in other bars.

The Cat House was cleaner than most bars I patronized. It was a classy place with a few cat touches. The feline influences were subtle things. There were paw prints, running the length of the bar, and a few more randomly leading to the restrooms. There were only two unisex bathrooms. Each one of them had a sign on the door that read 'Sandbox.' It was a clever idea but it wasn't as cute as the 'Birdbath' sign above the bar.

Everyone hooted and hollered when Gilda walked up on stage. It was just her, an acoustic guitar, a bar stool, and a little table for her drink. She was cool and confident on the stage. She looked amazing with her guitar, and a hand-rolled cigarette between her lips. I assumed it was a cigarette. I didn't really know if the Cat House was relaxed enough to let their people smoke the catnip on stage.

It didn't take long for Gilda to spot me in the crowd. She only looked at me for a second. She shot me a smile, and tucked her cigarette into the top string of her guitar, like a fucking rock star, and started into her first song.

She astonished me.

I made up my mind that I was going to leave before her set was over. Seeing her again made me want to frolic together in a field of flowers and vomit rainbows. I wanted to talked to her and tell her how much I loved her, and how I wanted to spend the rest of my days with her, but I knew it was a shit shute. I had left her in Nashville, before things could get serious, and she had returned the favor. The third try could have been a charm, but I wasn't willing to take my chances on it going South again.

I was just about to cut out, when she dedicated one of her songs. "This one is for that special guy, who might or might not be here tonight," she said.

The song didn't mention anyone by name, but she sang about falling in love from grave circumstances, and wanting nothing more than to drink wine and listen to records with her guy. It might have been vain, but I thought that the song might have been about me. I had always wanted a woman to write a song about me.

There was a chance that I was wrong, but it didn't matter if the song was for me, I didn't have anything to offer a woman like Gilda. I waited for her to start her next song, a song from Three Years Sober, and I made my exit. I wanted so badly to run back into the venue and sweep her off of the stage, but I knew she was destined for better things.

Alice was back in Indiana waiting for me to come home. I realized my place was at home with her, and a smarter guy would have driven back to the asshole of America, and lived out his happily ever after. I honestly loved Alice, but I loved Dara and Gilda, too.

The argument could have been made that I had fallen in love with every woman that gave me the time of day. That argument wouldn't be far from the truth, but I had fallen hardest for three very incredible women. Each of them were amazing in different ways, and all of them, especially Alice, deserved better than me.

35

When I returned home, Alice's car wasn't there. I wasn't sure if she was working, or how she had reacted to my disappearing act. I wouldn't have been surprised if she had packed her things and left my sorry ass. I was ready for nearly anything when I opened my front door. Not many things would have surprised me, but a baseball bat smashing into the wall next to my face took me completely off guard.

I had only stepped in the door, and set my suitcase down, before I heard a primal scream and saw the bat swing past my face. I wasn't fast enough to dodge the attack. My attacker was either just that bad at swinging a bat, or they weren't really sure they wanted to hit me.

My eyes followed the bat up as my attacker cocked it back to take another swing. I expected to see Alice wielding the wooded weapon of my destruction. She had every right to want to smash my face in, but to my surprise, the person holding the bat was shorter than Alice. My attacker was decked-out in knee high Dr. Martin boots, black pants, and a turtleneck and ski mask.

The boots gave her away, but the unmistakable sea-foam colored hair sticking out from under her mask was a dead give away.

I was just about to call Dara out on her horrible attempt to conceal her identity, when she took another swing. The second swing was more on target. It took nearly everything I had to dodge the assault. I dove back against the wall by the door, and watched the bat crash into my suitcase. The impact of the blow caused Dara to lose her grip on the bat, allowing me to spring forward and yank it out of her hand.

Once I had control of the bat, I wished I had let her keep it. It was a slightly less lethal weapon than the pistol she pulled out from behind her. I hadn't even noticed it tucked in the back of her pants, but it was unavoidable when she shoved it in my face.

"Dara, please, don't shoot me!" I yelled, "I'm really sorry that I hurt you, but if you shoot me, you will be fucking up your whole life. You don't want to do that!"

She didn't take the gun out of my face. "What the fuck? How did you know it was me?"

"Your hair is sticking out of your mask, but your boots gave you away."

"FUCK!"

Dara whipped her ski mask off and pushed the gun into my left cheek hard enough that I could feel the tip of the barrel breaking skin.

"I know you're pissed, but killing me is only going to lead to a shitstorm I don't want you to have to deal with."

"Who says I'm going to get caught? There are a hundred people lining up to kick your ass."

"That's probably true, but do you really want to take that chance? Do you want to spend the rest of your days looking over your shoulder, just hoping you got away with it?" I whimpered. "I've seen a few episodes of those crime scene investigation shows. They're pretty-"

"Shut up. SHUT UP! Just shut the fuck up!" She took the gun out of my face and covered her ears, while she backed away. "You always have something to say. Why do you always have to be so fucking cute?"

"It's a blessing and a curse."

Dara rushed toward me again, and shoved the gun into my mouth. "I told you to shut the fuck up. Don't make me shoot you!"

I didn't mumble another word. I was afraid that she might actually be crazy enough to pull the trigger. I couldn't really blame her if she blew my brains all over the wall. She might have even been doing society a favor, but I really didn't want to die, and I was pretty sure she didn't want to shoot me.

My suspicions were confirmed when she pulled the pistol out of my mouth, and said "I'm so fucking wet right now."

I had a number of smart-ass comments I could have added, but I kept my mouth shut, and thought about the nasty metallic flavor of the gun.

"Do you wanna feel?"

I was still afraid to speak.

Dara pressed the gun to my head, and asked again with more zeal. "I asked you if you want to feel how wet I am. Do you want to fuckin' touch it or not, asshole?"

"I always liked it when you were all wet down there, it's like Niagra Falls."

"You wanna touch me, Harlow?"

I thought of the best answer to save my life. "Yeah, I want to touch it,"

She kept the gun to my temple and moved my hand down her pants. She wasn't lying. She was wet, slick, and smooth. It brought back arousing memories, memories that made me harder than Chinese algebra.

Dara noticed my erection and worked her free hand into my jeans to tug at my dick. I wasn't the biggest fan of hand jobs, but with a gun pressed to my head, it seemed like the best idea in the room, and wasn't about to tell my gun wielding ex to stop.

I thought that play time was a nice way to lower the tension on the room, and took the moment to toss the bat on the floor. I hoped that she would take my action as a white flag, and drop the pistol. She didn't. She took it as another form of submission, prompting her to press the gun under my chin, stand on her tiptoes, and force her lips against mine.

She had always been an intense kisser, but with my fingers inside her, and a handgun between us, she was additionally tenacious. Her tongue darted in and out of my mouth, while she writhed on my hand within her panties. I kissed her back, and fingered her like I was trying to save my life.

I was terrified that Alice was going to walk in at any moment. I knew I was already in deep shit with her, and I knew fingering a gun-toting psycho in the apartment that we shared wasn't the best way to get back on her good side. I wanted to end things with Alice as peacefully as possible. Ultimately, I wanted to end everything, and still be alive at the end of it all.

Dara finally took the gun away from my head. "I love you."

"I still love you too, but this is some crazy shit."

"You still love me?"

"Of course I do. I just suck at the whole relationship thing."

"I suck too," Dara replied, with her hand still wrapped around my cock. "I don't know where we go from here. I want you so bad, but I have a pretty strong feeling that I fucked up any chances I might have ever had, when I pulled this gun on you."

"I'm not sure where we go from here either," I said moving my fingers inside her, to the rhythm of our conversation. "Trying to kill me repeatedly, and fucking up my car was not the best way to work things out."

"How did you know I was the one who fucked up your car and set your apartment on fire?"

"I didn't. I didn't have a clue, other than the green paint. Green is your favorite color," I laughed nervously. "I honestly didn't know until you just confirmed it for me."

"Shit! I guess I just narced myself out, huh?"

"Yeah, but that's all behind us now, as far as I'm concerned. I'm a little more worried about you trying to take my head off with that bat."

"That was pretty fucked up of me. I hope there's a way I can make it up to you."

"I don't know. You pulled a fucking gun on me."

Dara pulled her hand out of my pants. "I can at least try to make it up to you." She sat the gun down on the floor and knelt in front of me. I was already pretty close to getting off when she sat up on her knees to unzip my jeans and yanked them down to my ankles, but when she finally set the gun down, I nearly shot off from relief.

I nearly got off again as soon as my dick was in her mouth. Her lips and tongue moved around my cock with ruthless aggression, and as soon as she worked her hands into the action, I was finished. I tried to warn her, but I was already filling her mouth with the sweet tastes of release.

Dara didn't care that I came in her mouth. She liked it. She had always said that it was better to take a shot in the mouth than to have a bun in the oven.

She smiled while she licked her lips and fingers clean. I took it as my moment to move my foot over the pistol on the floor. I made sure to stand on it with most of my weight, in case she went to grab it again.

"Are you going to return the favor?"

Every bone in my body was telling me to say yes, but I couldn't. "I don't think that's going to happen."

"What? Why the fuck not?"

"I need to be honest with you. I do still have some serious feelings for you, and you are so fucking sexy that it pains me to say that we can't be together," I began. "I can't be with anyone. I need to focus on me and my shit. I'm not getting any younger, and it's time for me to get my shit together."

"I'm really happy that you've chosen this moment to finally grow up. Wow! Congradu-fucking-lations!"

"Dara, you destroyed my car, set my apartment on fire, tried to kill me with a baseball bat, and shoved a gun in my mouth, and I'm still willing to be friends. I think that's pretty fucking cool of me. I'm not saying we might not have a chance down the road, but I need to focus right now, and you might want to deal with some of your own shit, too. I'm not suggesting professional help, but it might not be a bad idea."

"I'm not fucking crazy, Harlow!"

"That's exactly what a crazy person would say. I'm not even saying you're crazy, but admitting you might have a problem is the first step. I don't know the rest of the steps. I've never made it past the first one, but let's stop the property damage, arson, and attacking people with random weapons, and see where things go from there, cool?"

"I know," Dara laughed. "You're right. I might have overacted a little."

"See, now, doesn't that feel better?"

"It doesn't feel as good as you fingering me. Can we just go back to that part? I promise not to fuck up anything else, or try to kill you again."

"Trust me, that sounds like a sweet offer, but I have some things I need to sort out here first. Why don't you take your gun, and your bat, and head home, and I'll get ahold of you after I deal with my Alice situation? Is that fair?"

Dara stood up and gave me a big hug and a deep kiss. "That's more than fair."

When she pulled away from the kiss, I saw the front door of the apartment swing open. Alice was standing there with her briefcase in one hand, and a couple bags of groceries in the other. She looked more confused than pissed off.

It had to be awkward for her to see a strange girl, with green hair, kissing me while my pants were still around my ankles, spent dick and all.

Alice didn't say anything. She just stood there and took the whole thing in. She just watched as Dara picked up her bat and started to leave.

I picked up the pistol and tossed it to Dara. "Don't forget your gun."

Dara caught the gun and walked past Alice, without event. "Bye."

Alice watched Dara leave, but her jaw dropped as she turned her attention back to me. I could tell she had a million questions, and that she had moved past furious. She had moved back to that calm sort of angry, the really scary kind of angry.

I covered myself, and moved slowly as I pulled up my pants. I could see that Dara had made it out to her beat-up blue van, and was on her way out of my life again. I knew talking to Alice wasn't going to be easy, but the interaction with Dara made it even more fucked-up.

I was happy that Dara had taken the gun and baseball bat with her.

"Hi, honey," I smiled nervously at Alice. "I think we need to talk."

36

I swore that I'd never go to another wedding, but when Abby got remarried, I didn't really have a choice.

While Abby was out making bad choices, she hooked up with a singer-songwriter, Slate Skinner from St. Louis. They shared a few whiskey drinks after a show, and before either of them knew it, they were in love. She took her books on tour to the cities he was going to be in, and they did their writing on the road together.

I was all happy for her, until she told me that she was getting remarried, and that she wanted me to stand up with her. I was given the title of Bridesman, because I stood up with Abby, and Silvia, the groom's sexy sister, was dubbed the Groomsmaid. This was just one of the unusual things about the wedding. The fact that it wasn't a traditional wedding was one of the only reasons I agreed to the shit. Abby also knew that an open bar would hook me, and if I didn't get too drunk during the reception, I might have something to write about, when it was over.

I was walking out of the storage room, near the back of the club the wedding was in. I was happy that the wedding wasn't in a church. I didn't feel bad about fucking a bridesmaid in the church at Destiny's wedding, but the storage room of the club was much nicer. It was full of old furniture and cases of alcohol.

Being in Abby's wedding also meant seeing a few of the same people from Destiny's wedding again. I wasn't sure who all of their mutual friends were, but it was weird to see some of them again, after I had made such an ass out of myself the last time.

Seeing Destiny was the hardest part. I was happy that her stupid husband didn't come with her, but it wouldn't have mattered if he had. All of my feelings for Destiny were long gone, and we didn't talk much. We spoke, but it seemed like it physically hurt her to speak to me. I didn't really care either way.

Silvia was very into the idea of getting high, and getting naked. I wasn't above hooking up at the wedding. I was single, and I had never had sex with a groomsmaid before. I was also sure that a little sex, drugs, and rock 'n' roll made every wedding better.

I even waited for Silvia to come out of the storage room, before I headed back to the wedding party table.

While I waited for Silvia, I watched people mingling around the reception, and just enjoyed the music. The age of the disc jockey was dead. Everyone had an iPod or some kind of MP3 player. A lot of things pissed me off about weddings, but one of my biggest pet peeves was the iJ. There were no more Djs. There wasn't any skill involved in playing music for a party anymore. Playing a set wasn't about the timing of the next song, or making sure you brought the right mix of music for the crowd. It was all about having 39474 songs on one device, and a playlist that just played while the guy with the mic collected a fat check. It was bullshit in my opinion.

I expected more from a so-called recording artist's wedding.

When it was time to toss the bouquet, Abby came to find the groomsmaid and me, because it was taking Slivia forever to get dressed. There really wasn't any hiding what we had been up to, either. Abby was hip to what had gone down at Destiny's wedding, and Silvia was something of a stoner-slut, according to Abby.

After a while, Abby eventually went to toss the bouquet without us, leaving me to talk to some random drunk guy.

"I think it was Oscar Wilde that said: 'Marriage is a great institution for people who like institutions,'" he slurred.

"That's funny, but that was actually Groucho Marx. It's from the movie Animal Crackers," I scoffed. "Oscar Wilde said: 'Bigamy is having one wife too many. Monogamy is the same.' He also said "How can a woman be expected to be happy with a man who insists on treating her as if she were a perfectly normal human being."

"Who cares, weddings suck."

"I agree. I promised myself that I'd never go to another one of these fucking things, and I swore I'd never be in another one."

The drunk guy just kept getting louder. "What changed your mind?"

"I'm still not sure. I think they got me with the promise of free booze again."

"Getting to walk down the aisle with that sexy woman can't be all bad, either," he said. "Did you see the tits on her?"

"I might have noticed her boobs, but I've been pretty busy," I laughed.

"I might take a run at that."

"I think you should give it the old college try. You don't stand a chance, but you should still try."

I opened the storage room door and shoved my new drunk friend inside. I had had enough of him, but I felt like tossing him a bone. I seriously doubted that Silvia would mind. I thought the whole thing was pretty funny, until a familiar voice broke up the party.

"I never thought I'd see you at another wedding," a voice said from behind me.

I turned around to see Alice standing there. She had put on a few pounds, and cut her hair, but she still looked incredible. I couldn't even remember how long it had been since the last time I had seen her. I knew the moment I saw her standing there that I had missed her. The very sight of her made my heart leap into my throat.

"Oh! Wow! I never thought I'd see you-"

"Save it. You made your choice. I haven't seen you in months, and now here you are. Some things never change."

I knew that I had blown a good thing with Alice. She was one of the keepers, but I still wasn't ready to grow up and be the man she needed in her life. And it didn't change the fact that I had done wrong by her.

I stammered to find the right words. "I can explain."

"I said I didn't want to know. I'm just happy to see you alive. I thought you might have-"

"I am really sorry. I felt like a dick for weeks."

"Just a few weeks. It's a shame it didn't last longer. I thought you were a dick for longer than that. I might still harbor that opinion."

"I can understand that," I mumbled. "How are you?"

"I'm good, really good."

"You look good."

Alice laughed. "Bullshit. I look like a house. I keep

gaining weight, and it's only going to get worse."

"I don't get it. What do you mean? You look-"

"I'm fucking pregnant. I'm about 32 weeks along. How's your math?"

"Are you saying the baby is mine?"

"No, Harlow. The baby is mine. We don't need you in our lives to fuck shit up. I survived your shit, and I've come this far without you, I think I can handle being a single mom."

"Are you sure there-"

"I'm sure! I loved you, you asshole," Alice yelled. "Don't even ask if there was anyone else. I wanted you. I thought we would make it. I was wrong."

"I don't know what to say."

"Say goodbye. That's all that is left to say.. We don't need you."

I didn't say goodbye, and Alice didn't give me the chance. She just walked away. She didn't even look back.

My gut was swirling with uncomfortable excitement. I wasn't wanted, but I was still going to be a father. I wasn't sure if there was any way to get into the kid's life, or if it was even a good idea to try, but there was only one thing to do.

I grabbed a bottle of something off of the table next to me and started drinking. It was wine. I didn't care what year it was, what kind it was, or what valley the grapes had been plucked from. It was wet, and it had alcohol in it. That was all I needed.

I was still trying to figure out my next move when the groomsmaid finally walked out of the storage room. She was adjusting herself in her strapless dress, and trying to figure out why I looked so serious. She wasn't even trying to hide what had just happened behind closed doors. She was classy like that.

She walked straight over to me. "We definitely

have to do that again."

"No, you don't need me."

"Huh? What does that mean?" Silvia asked, "Just for the record, I think there was some drunk guy passed out in there the whole time. He's asleep inside the door."

"That's for sure."

"Are you even listening to me?"

"Nothing."

"What?"

I walked away, leaving the Silvia standing there all frustrated and confused. It didn't matter to me. She didn't matter.

In that moment, I knew that I finally had a reason to pull my shit together. I needed to be the best me I could be, not for myself, not for any woman, but because I was going to be a father. I wanted to be a better father than my dad, and his dad before him. I was going to be the best damn dad I could be.

Alice didn't want anything to do with me, but I still loved her. I was pretty sure that I would always love her. I would fuck things up a million more times, but she would always be the one I would want to run back to, and she would forever be the mother of my child.

In the end, there was only Alice.

25121712R00137

Made in the USA
Lexington, KY
14 August 2013